A JACK NOVAK DETECTIVE NOVEL

MURDER ON THE DOUBLE

REG IVORY

1

H omes Kinney walked into the living room of the Roswell, Georgia, apartment and office he shared with his longtime detective partner, Jack Novak. Novak was cleaning his father's .45, a regular weekly chore. The two men both needed shaves badly.

"Jack, you doing anything right now?" Homes asked.

Novak held up the gun and waved it.

"I mean after that." Homes seated himself across from Novak.

"Okay," Jack said, putting the pistol aside. "What's going on?"

"Two things. Captain Taylor called me this morning and asked me to have lunch. Do you remember him ever asking me – or you – to have lunch when we were on the Roswell force?"

"Never. You are either in deep shit and you're going to lose your pension or he wants you to pick up the check."

"That's what I thought, so I asked him. He said he was buying. Then he told me why."

Novak waited. He looked at his best friend and spread out his arms and hands. "So?"

Homes took a deep breath. "You weren't on the force when the Carstairs murder case hit the Roswell area."

"That's right. You told me you were the lead detective and that it was never solved."

Homes nodded. "Because I never could solve it. The only case I wasn't able to solve in over twenty years on the Roswell police force."

"So why is the Cap calling you? Is this the anniversary of the murder or something?"

Homes shook his head. "No. As you know, a murder case is never closed. It may go cold – like this one. But it's never closed."

"Right. So why – "

"You know we didn't have any solid DNA evidence collection and testing back then," Homes said.

Novak cleared his throat. "Wait a minute. Hold it. You're not going to tell me what I know you're going to tell me, are you?"

"I am. The FBI is offering a grant to help local PDs solve some cold murder cases. They sent Roswell a few preliminary tests they ran on the Carstairs murder evidence that looked promising. You know they can still ID those things nowadays, no matter how old it is."

Novak threw down the rag he had been cleaning the gun with and pushed his chair back from the table. "Homes, for God's sake, you don't need this. You're too old for this shit. More important, you have over a million bucks in diamonds, you have a beautiful girlfriend thirty years younger than you are who's nuts about you. Go count your diamonds in that fish tank sitting over there. It damn near killed both of us to get them. Why would you want to – "

"Because it's my fault the murder was never solved," Homes said. "It's my damn fault and it's bugged me for the last 20 years."

"Homes, I know you and NOTHING bugs you," Novak said. "Go have a beer, call Diane and forget about this."

"I can't. I've tried."

Novak sat back down. "So what do you want from me?"

"I want you to go with me to have lunch with the Cap and help me out with the case."

Novak threw up his hands. "Homes, we've been best friends for fifteen years. I thought you liked me, other than that time you shot me, of course. But I've mostly forgotten that which is what you should do about this whole cold case business."

"I shot you to save your life, as you well know, and I'd do it again. I mean, to save your life, not to just shoot you. You tackle a case with everything you've got and that's what I need from someone I trust. And you've got that "in" with the head of the local FBI here in Atlanta and we may need that kind of help digging into the evidence."

"Correct me if I'm wrong, but isn't your girlfriend one of the top FBI agents in the Atlanta office? Why can't she help you?"

"She can and she will. But I need you, too. Besides, that's the second thing I want to talk to you about."

"The FBI?"

"No. About Diane." Homes paused for a moment; his eyes lowered. "I'm going to ask her to marry me."

Jack was stunned. Homes had been a bachelor all his adult life and vowed he would never marry.

"Homes, this is the first time I've wanted a drink since I swore off five years ago. You're serious?"

Homes nodded. "Yep."

"So why are you telling me this. Do you want my blessing or some damned thing?"

`No. I want to know if it's okay if Diane moves in here with us after she and I get married."

Novak just stared at his friend for a moment and then started laughing. Homes joined in until they were both sitting on the floor, their laughter turning to tears.

2

"So what did you think?" Homes asked as they left the Roswell restaurant.

Jack placed the evidence box he was carrying in the back seat of the car. "Well, I did notice that the Cap let me pick up the check, when you said he was paying. By the way, isn't it illegal to remove evidence boxes from police headquarters?"

"Yes it is. And the Cap just invited me for lunch, not the two of us. Thanks for carrying out the evidence box while I talked to Ben Hector. He told me he just got divorced."

Jack started the car and headed for their home office. "I thought I heard that about Hector from someone. Does that spook you about asking Diane to marry you?"

"Not at all. Why would she ever want to get divorced?" Homes said.

"Well, you drink a lot of beer and you're thirty years older than she is. What if she meets a younger guy?"

"She meets younger guys all the time. I never worry about them."

"You never worry about anything," Jack said, "except this damn old murder case."

"Which I'm going to solve if it kills me."

"Glad you didn't say 'kills us.' I've had enough close calls. How do you want to handle this?"

"Let's dig into the box when we get home and make a plan."

"Will this be one of your plans or mine?"

"Yours of course. I'm not good at planning. Only solving murders."

"How long have we been at this?" Homes said. Papers and photographs were scattered all over the living room table. Novak had been taking notes on a yellow pad.

"Almost three hours. You look like you need a beer."

"Just what I was thinking," Homes said, getting up and walking into the kitchen. "What do you think so far?"

"It was good going over all the details you never told me about. Let's see if I get this straight. Wendy Carstairs was murdered about twenty years ago by a person or persons unknown. Brutally murdered, I have to say, after reading the descriptions of her body and seeing the photos from the autopsy. I didn't remember that she had been decapitated and her body stabbed – was it seventeen times?"

"Something like that," Homes said. "Only her head was found in a Roswell dumpster, which is how our department got involved. The Carstairs had an apartment here and a condo in Atlanta where the rest of the body was found."

"By the way, Wendy was a real knockout from the formal photo of her with her husband that was also in the evidence box."

"That she was," Homes said. "You weren't around here then. I think you were still in Iraq trying to save the world from democracy."

"I think you got that wrong," Jack said, smiling.

"Whatever. Wendy Carstairs was the toast of this town. She and her hubby, Duane, were very rich and loved living the good life. They were seen everywhere and did everything. Sponsored events, gave to charities, held elegant dances that were the social events of every season."

"What did her husband do?"

"Good question. COO of the Breckenridge Corporation. He was involved in investments was all we could find out at the time. The newspaper never tracked down exactly what they were and there were rumors of drug involvement and even illegal weapons sales. The husband made a lot of trips to many countries in the Middle East and South America, among others. Mexico more than any other place. I think those are angles we should explore."

"Agreed," Jack said. "Was it a happy marriage?"

"As far as anyone knew it was. But what we found out during the murder investigation was that Wendy was – shall we say – not always on her best behavior."

"She was screwing around."

"All around. And around. With some very well-known men on our sports teams, in entertainment and other businesses. It seems she was particularly fond of Black athletes. And, it is alleged, involved with several women, as well."

"I love it when you use big words like *alleged*. Did you have to look it up?"

"Yeah. I checked it in the dictionary when I was in the bathroom."

"This autopsy report mentions that Wendy had had sex recently," Jack said. "It also says there were significant amounts of drugs in her system but they're still working on identifying what they were."

"That's where the FBI will come in handy. I'd like to know if the semen they found on her clothing and on her body could be identified in any current databases, as well as the kinds of drugs she was using."

Jack nodded. "Good thinking. What about her husband Duane?"

"Apparently, Duane and Wendy had an understanding because we found out he was doing pretty much the same thing she was doing. He was particularly fond of prostitutes."

"Any problems with that? Did they ever have any arguments about their – um – arrangements?"

"That would be investigative point number two or three," Homes said. "Actually, we thought the husband was good for the murder but we had no proof."

"Any chance he's still around?"

"Only his body, which is in Oakland cemetery downtown. He died about ten years ago under what was described as mysterious circumstances. Maybe we should exhume the body. Oh, I already have a list of people they knew who still live in the area."

"Exhume. That's two big words in the same conversation. Hey, you're getting pretty good at this detective stuff," Jack said. "Maybe you don't need me. I assume you followed up on most of these trails during the first investigation?"

"Yes. I busted my ass, along with other guys on my team, but we didn't come up with diddly squat."

"Is that a professional detective term?"

Homes snickered. "I'm a lot funnier than you are, Jack. You should stick with seducing every woman in the Roswell/Alpharetta area, to say nothing of downtown Atlanta."

Jack ignored him. "So we need to talk to whomever is left around here that knew the Carstairs and see if we can stir the pot."

"Right. Twenty years is a long time. But the FBI analysis may come up with some new information. Some of the people we interview might also be ready to talk."

"Agreed," Jack said. "By the way, have you asked Diane the big question yet?"

"You mean if she's still a virgin? I know the answer to that."

"No, you idiot. The marriage question."

"Oh, that," Homes said. "I'm biding my time. I want to ask her after I solve this big case and she's so impressed she agrees to marry me without thinking too hard about it."

"A wise move, my friend. Let's get started on this list of names."

3

"You should have been MVP that year," Novak said to the slightly grey-ing Black man stretched out on the sofa in his Atlanta penthouse. A golden baseball bat inside an attractive mahogany case hung on the wall above him.

"Yeah, I was the most valuable for the Braves that year but that bastard Stanton on the Phillies beat me out. He hit more home runs but I had more RBIs. Neither one of our teams made the Series, though." He sighed a little. "You never forget all that shit no matter how many years go by," he said.

"No Braves fan will ever forget Rudy Simmons," Novak said. "I still have your baseball card somewhere."

Simmons smiled and swiveled his feet from the couch to the floor. "Yeah, I haven't paid for a drink in the last fifteen years no matter what bar I hit. And I've hit them all. Speaking of drinks, how about a beer?" He stood up and walked toward his kitchen.

"No thanks. I had to give it up," Novak said.

"Ulcers?" Simmons asked

"No, strangely enough I never got ulcers. But I had damn near every-thing else before I hit bottom."

"Know what you mean. I had a few teammates who had that problem." Simmons walked back and sat down on the sofa. "So you want me to tell you about my relationship" – he drew out the word into four distinct syllables, then he laughed. "Why the hell does everything men and women do together have to be a *re-la-tion-ship?* Why can't they just have a good time screwing around for a while?"

"Is that what the two of you were doing?"

"Yeah man. That was it. She was great in the sack and she looked like a million bucks. I was who I was and it made her feel good to be seen with me. I had lots of women. Still do. She liked athletes. Especially Black athletes. Make sure you talk to Booster Desmond, the old center for the Hawks. Boost and Wendy had a thing going for a while. It was no big deal to her. Or to me."

Novak nodded. "So, no love match, huh?"

"No. None of that shit. Neither of us needed or wanted that. She went through plenty of men but she always came back to Rudy Simmons whenever she wanted some real action."

"It didn't bother you that she was married?"

"Not a bit. Why should it? It didn't bother her and it sure as hell never bothered her husband." Simmons took a swig of his beer. "What the hell was his name?"

"Duane," Novak said.

"Yeah, that's it. Dopey Duane she used to call him. No, he never bothered either of us. He was doin' his own thing. Hookers mostly. So what brought this sorry mess up again?"

"Roswell PD got a federal grant through the FBI to dig into their unsolved murder files and see if they couldn't come up with some answers. The Carstairs case still bugs people."

"Hell, it never bugged me. All I can tell you is that I didn't kill the bitch. I was having too much fun with her. And so were a lot of other guys in this town. I remember when all that murder shit hit the papers. Somebody must have really hated Wendy to do all that stuff they described in the papers. You can check me out, Novak. I wasn't even in town. We had a game in Pittsburgh that day she was killed. I hit two home runs. Hey, you want to see the gold .45 the team gave me when I retired?""

"Sure." They walked over to a gleaming black case on the wall. Inside was a shiny gold-plated .45 automatic. "That case is made out of African Blackwood, man," Rudy said. "And that .45 works, too. Only the best for Simmons."

"Nice, man. I've never seen one like it. Anybody else you can think of that I should talk to besides Booster?" They sat back down.

"I ain't got enough paper to make a list of names that long," Simmons said, smiling. "That chick was really somethin.' Just concentrate on Atlanta sports stars from that period and you'll stay busy."

Novak stood up. "I'll leave you my card in case you think of something that might help. It was great talking baseball with you, Rudy. You're still the best to a lot of us in Atlanta."

Simmons stood up and shook hands with Jack. "It's always good to hear somebody who remembers you from the old days. Come back any time."

4

"**A**lice Townsend? Didn't they call her Blue Alice cause she sang the blues so sweet?"

Novak was back in the office portion of their apartment with Homes sitting across from him.

"Exactly right," Homes said. "Ever hear her?"

"No. Before my time. Read about her in the papers. So she's still around?"

"Yeah. Got an apartment in Buckhead. Doesn't sing much anymore but she might talk to you," Homes said. "Tell her you're a Bobby Darin fan. You two are the only people in town who knows who the hell he was. Maybe that'll open the door. I've got a couple of her old albums if you're interested. Man, that lady could sing."

"Why do you want me to interview her?"

"You do better with women."

"Glad to hear you're finally admitting it," Jack said, looking at the witness sheet Homes had typed up. "I'll give her a call and set up a meeting. I'll try for dinner at Nikolai's Roof. She might like that."

Homes whistled. "She'd be a damn fool not to. "Think the expense account can handle it?"

"That's what being a millionaire is all about," Novak said, reaching across to the fish tank and patting its sides as the little golden fins glided by the shimmering diamonds covering the bottom.

"How about digging those old albums out for me?"

◆ ◆ ◆

"You don't drink champagne?" Alice Townsend sipped from her flute and smiled at Novak. "And thank you for suggesting Nikolai's for dinner. They are the only restaurant that can prepare Fugu properly. It's my favorite meal."

Jack had been admiring the lovely woman through dinner. Her album covers didn't do her justice. In her mid-40s, her long ebony hair fell softly across her shoulders. Her mouth was soft and pleasant to watch as she spoke.

"Alcohol gives me a headache," he said. "Actually, it damn near killed me, so I quit."

She nodded. "I seem to recall a few stories about you in the Constitution over the years. You had some close calls. Glad you got past the problem."

"Well, like they say, I take it one day at a time. By the way, my partner, Homes Kinney, gave me a few of your albums. You have a great voice."

She lifted her glass to him. "I still get out and sing those blues every once in a while. Do you know the Dorset Club downtown? Small, quiet joint in lower Buckhead. I wanted a place I could call my own so I bought it. I know some big names in the business that like to sing in a small, intimate setting. We seat only fifty. I had Tony Bennett in there last year. We sang a duet. *Love For Sale.*"

"Wow. I know the name of the club but haven't been down there yet. I'll make it a point to see you the next time you appear. My email is on the card I gave you. I'd appreciate a reminder."

"Glad to do it. You're an interesting man, Novak. That's aside from the murder investigation you're into." She smiled again. "Are you going to slap the cuffs on me now?"

Jack returned her smile. "I thought I'd wait until after dessert. I'm just trying to find a few answers about the Carstairs murder. Anything come to mind that might help us?"

Alice took another sip. "I know a lot about Wendy Carstairs. Why don't we go back to my place and I'll tell you all about it?"

Townsend's penthouse apartment had been featured in several Sunday editions of the Constitution, the New York Times, and many architectural magazines as well. Novak had no decorating taste but even he could appreciate the elegance of the furniture and the original art throughout the place. He was impressed.

"Make yourself comfortable," Alice said. "I'll be right back. There are some soft drinks in the fridge. Help yourself."

Jack wandered into the kitchen and looked around. The area was every bit as luxurious as the rest of the apartment. A mahogany rack of fine glassware lined one wall as well as more artwork that blended in perfectly.

"You won't find any Picassos in there," Alice said, walking back into the living room. She had changed into what looked like a silk short-sleeved jogging outfit and was barefoot. "Let's sit over here." She gestured to an elegant sofa. "All my furniture is Michael Amani. I love Italians," she said. "I'm going to have a little cognac. Will that bother you?" She filled a small glass from a decanter.

"Not at all," Novak said, sitting down as she walked over and sat beside him, tucking her long shapely legs beneath her.

"You're well-known as a good detective so I'm assuming you've read a little of my history. Wendy Carstairs and I had many things in common. She liked to live well and enjoy life and so did I." She paused, sipped her cognac, and looked at Jack. "We gradually found out that we enjoyed each other on a very personal level. That lasted for – oh – a little over a year. The truth is that I fell in love with Wendy and that scared her off. I was a little depressed for a while after we split but some friends said it gave even more of a subtlety to my voice when I sang the blues."

Jack nodded as she sipped her drink again. "My research also turned up the fact that Wendy played the field with both men and women. Did that ever disturb you?"

"Looking for a motive, I see. Not a bit. Wendy and I had our own thing and it was good for both of us. I was actually surprised when the physical attraction happened. That was not something I had been into and it's never happened again. She was unique for me."

"She seemed to be attracted to several Atlanta athletes," Jack said.

"Yes. She introduced me to a few. I don't know sports very well, but there was a baseball player and one of the basketball men. I found them arrogant but Wendy obviously liked them. The baseball player was particularly fond of her."

Jack took his time with his next question. "Ever get jealous about the other men – or women – in her life?"

Alice continued smiling and put her glass down. "Jealousy was never a part of our relationship. We never argued. When Wendy and I were together it was like we were in our own private world. What happened outside that world was unimportant." She paused a minute, staring at Novak, her dark dusky eyes absorbing his every feature. "Now, are we going to keep on talking about a dead woman from the past? I think it's about time you kissed me."

5

"So how did it go with Alice?" Homes said as the partners had lunch the next day.

"It went well," Jack said. "She's quite a woman."

"That's what you always say when something's going on. You haven't come home that early in the morning in quite some time."

Jack chuckled. "You sound just like my mother. Are you still going to watch out for me when you get married?"

"No. I'll be busy with other duties. So what have we learned about this case so far?"

"Not a hell of a lot," Jack said. "No one I've talked to admits any problems in their relationships with Wendy Carstairs. They all say the sex was great and nobody ever got jealous of the competition."

"And you believe that?"

"Not a damn bit," Novak said. "Somebody's lying; Maybe everybody. What about your interviews?"

"Same thing. I got nothing but sexy stories. Wendy Carstairs must have been quite – entertaining. We need to shake something loose. Any ideas?"

"A few," Jack said. "What about the diary routine?"

"What diary?"

"The Wendy Carstairs diary we just found where she names names."

"But we didn't . . . oh, I get it. THAT diary."

"We tell people about the nonexistent diary we just found, tell them Wendy revealed intimate details about them and see who starts flinching and making up alibis."

Homes couldn't keep from laughing. "We used this on the Remington case, didn't we?

I remember we almost had five people ready to confess before we found the guilty one."

"That's right," Jack said. "I don't expect that to happen this time but you never know what might turn up. Who's next on your list?"

"Maxine Turner. She was assistant COO to Duane Carstairs when he ran the Breckenridge Corporation. Now she's the boss."

"Do we know yet what kind of business Breckenridge was involved in?" Jack said.

"That's what I'm going to ask her. As I said, no one knew what they did twenty years ago. Their incorporation documents use a lot of five syllable words about buying and selling but they don't describe exactly what."

"Good. See what you can dig out of her. Use the diary thing if you think it will help. Let's see if we can break something loose."

◆ ◆ ◆

"I really don't understand why you're speaking to me, Mr. – is it Kinsey?" Maxine Turner looked Homes over disapprovingly.

Homes had been studying her carefully. Perhaps in her early 50s, she had gray-streaked hair pulled back into a tight bun. Pencil thin eyebrows. Her mouth formed what looked like a straight line where her lips should be. She was dressed in an extremely conservative way in a high-collard black dress with a gray smock with wide pockets and a Breckenridge logo.

"It's Kinney. Homes Kinney," he said. "As I explained, my partner and I are working in cooperation with the FBI and the Atlanta and Roswell police departments – all through a federal grant aimed at clearing unsolved cases. I can show you my credentials again if you like."

Turner waved her hand at the detective, as if to dismiss the whole subject. "I only met Wendy Carstairs briefly a few times. I knew Mr. Carstairs – Duane – quite well. We worked together for several years and I learned a lot from him. He was quite a mentor. Probably a genius in his field. He is still very much missed." She glanced out the window of her well-appointed office, tears in her eyes. A large painting of Duane Carstairs looked down at her from the wall above.

"And just exactly what field was that?" Homes asked.

The woman stared at him a moment. "Investments," she said, and began to shuffle papers on her desk. "I'm very busy and I think this interview is over."

Homes had been waiting for this. "That's fine with me, Ms. Turner. You have the choice of answering my questions here or speaking to the FBI when they arrive tomorrow. I can promise you they'll be a lot more aggressive than I've been and will probably take you directly to their offices just a few blocks from here."

She glared at him and cleared her throat. "Precisely what is it you want to know?"

Homes cleared his throat too. "I'm not supposed to release this but I'll tell you this much. We've found an old diary of Wendy's. She writes about Duane's business and mentions you and others several times and what your real duties were here at Breckenridge. What I want to know is what the hell kind of business are you running here and I mean specifically? We can and will subpoena your records if that's necessary. I also want to know if you have any information as to who might have killed Wendy Carstairs." He smiled and waited.

The woman's face had become bright red. "It certainly wasn't me. You'll need a subpoena and you can ask your questions through my attorney," she said, standing up.

"You can absolutely contact your attorney but that won't affect the FBI. They'll get their own subpoenas, walk in, empty your files, and remove your computers. Have a nice day."

Homes pushed his chair back and left the office.

6

"**From now on I'm leaving the interviews with females to you**," Homes said as he sat in the office portion of their detective agency.

Novak looked up from the DNA analysis report he had been reading. "And why is that?"

"Just because you do better with women, especially the older ones."

"Maxine Turner must have been tough," Novak said, smiling.

"Frosty and uncooperative. Dresses like an old lady. She didn't seem that sharp to me. She did think Duane Carstairs was a genius, though. Several pictures of him on her desk and she was getting misty-eyed as she talked about him. Might be something there. I'll let the Feds deal with her. By the way, I used the diary thing and it obviously upset her. That may develop into something. What's been going on here?"

Jack held up the paper. "Here's something that may end this whole case. It's the DNA report on the semen stains and other clues they found on Wendy Carstairs body and clothing. Are you ready for this?"

"Hit me with it," Homes said.

"It seems there were two different semen samples in or on Wendy's body. One is from her husband. The other is from our friend Rudy Simmons."

"The ballplayer?"

"Right. And there's more. Some hairs collected from her clothing and body are from an unidentified female, and they're still working on IDing them. I'm guessing they belong to Alice Townsend. Finally, the drugs in her system included heroin, cocaine, and some other exotic stuff they're still puzzling over. Not in doses enough to kill her but pretty significant. I'm guessing she was high when she was murdered."

"Wow. Two different semen stains and some female hairs. Sounds like Wendy had a busy night."

"One last thing," Novak said. "At the time, the FBI was able to freeze most of her stomach contents, thinking they might be able to identify them in the future. Their guys did a good job of IDing the mixture. Seems she had eaten a good portion of Fugu."

"And what the hell might that be?"

Novak had to laugh. "You'd think your Vietnamese girlfriend might have turned you on to Fugu by now. It's a Japanese fish dish – a real delicacy in Southeast Asia."

"Diane likes hamburgers. So why is this interesting?"

"Two reasons. Fugu happens to be extremely poisonous unless it is prepared properly and it is also our blues singer, Alice Townsend's, favorite meal."

Homes shook his head. "Tell me why anyone would eat a poisonous fish."

"Alice told me it is simply one of the most delicious foods she has ever tasted."

"Until it kills you," Homes said, laughing. "So, let's see where this puts us. We have a woman who was apparently stabbed to death and decapitated, who also had large amounts of drugs in her system, and who had eaten poisonous fish. We also know that she had sex with at least two men and one woman. Tell me, Jack, have you figured out who murdered her yet?"

"Sure. I'm just keeping it to myself to piss you off."

"I knew you were going to say that. I'm still betting on her dead husband."

"Trouble with that is, it will be damned difficult to prove he's the guy now that he's dead."

Homes sighed. "Right. But at least I'll get some satisfaction out of knowing who did it. What's next?"

Jack picked up a yellow pad. "Does the name Audrey Taylor remind you of anything?"

"No, I don't think so."

"How about her – uh – professional name - Kitten Claws?"

Homes smiled. "Now you've got me interested. I arrested Kitten three or four times and we became – uh – friends. I had forgotten her real name."

"Why Homes," Jack said facetiously, "I never knew you befriended any ladies of the night."

"Well, she was a great CI. Helped me solve quite a few cases."

"And I'm sure you and your confidential informant had to work many late nights keeping crime at bay in Roswell."

"Hey, we protect and serve," Homes said, laughing. "Tell you what. How about letting me take Kitten. I can probably get more out of her than you can."

"I have no doubt about that at all," Jack said, throwing a couch pillow at his partner. "Want her yellow sheet from her old file?"

"I won't need that. I've got it memorized."

7

Kitten Claws' apartment was not far from the detective's office in Roswell. Homes smiled thinking about her as he drove the mile or two to her place. She was quite a woman in the old days and he wondered how she had turned out. He found no current information on her in the Roswell PD files except her address and an old photograph. People think that most hookers aren't attractive. But Kitten – he called her Kit – put a lie to that. She was 19 when he met her and had been a beauty queen and star athlete in high school. Smart as hell, too. They had talked for hours about life in general and he never could figure out why she stayed in her chosen profession. He remembered she had gotten into drugs, was arrested more often, and then disappeared.

Her apartment was in a fairly new area of Roswell, more expensive than Homes had expected to find. He rang the bell and waited, wondering if they would reconnect. A well-dressed young man answered the door.

"Can I help you?"

Homes introduced himself, showed his credentials, and asked if he could speak to Ms. Taylor.

"Oh, that's my mom. She's Mrs. Carrie now." He turned his head and raised his voice. "Mom, there's someone here to see you. I'm headed out to play a little basketball. See you later."

Homes almost didn't recognize her when she walked into the hallway. In his twenty years as a cop, he had met many women like Kit. Kids who got a bad start for some reason and gradually wore themselves out over the years. She would be almost forty now. Looked about 25 to him.

"My God. Homes, is that you?" she said and walked up to him and hugged him. "You look the same except for the gray hair and maybe a few extra pounds."

Homes smiled. "And I have to say you look great, Kit. I didn't know – "

She nodded. "You didn't know how I might have turned out, what I would look like. Come in and sit down."

They walked into the nicely furnished living room and sat across from each other. Homes just stared at her. "So bring me up to date. The last I heard about you –" He stopped, not knowing how to put what he wanted to say.

"It's okay. I know what's going through your head. Oh, by the way, please call me Audrey if my kid's around. His name is Jerry. He knows I was no angel but not exactly what my occupation was in the old days."

"Sure. Don't worry about me. So what are you doing now?"

"You'll get a kick out of this, Homes. I'm a counselor at a drug rehab center. Actually have a master's degree in psychology." She paused for a minute. "Surprised?"

"A little," he said. "You were always smart – smart enough to do what you've done. I never could figure out why you didn't get out of the life and start over."

"Yeah, that was a tough thing to do. The drugs complicated it even more. I had to go into rehab and meet the right guy there. Name was Tommy Carrie. Did you ever know him?"

Homes shook his head. "Not that I can recall."

"We actually were in high school together but never really knew each other. He's the one that got me on the right track. We fell in love. Got married. Jerry came along. Maybe this sounds like a cliché to you but it never was for me. I worked hard at all of it."

"Do you and Tommy still work together?"

Audrey looked down and folded her hands. "Tommy was killed about ten years ago by an addict at our rehab center. The kid was higher than hell and stabbed him. It happened so fast. I think that was a real test for me. There I was with a ten-year-old kid, no husband, and no money. I thought about getting high or screwing up my life some other way. I decided to keep my head in the game – being a mother and a counselor – and do the best I could. Some friends helped. It's been tough sometimes but it's been a good life."

"I'm impressed, Kit. I mean Audrey. You sure as hell aren't Kit anymore. No new man in your life?"

"Thanks. No, no one special. I don't know if there ever will be. So, why are you here, Homes? I'm clean, I swear," she said, laughing.

Homes explained the cold case he was working on and that her name was found in an old police file when she had been arrested for prostitution along with Duane Carstairs, Wendy's husband. Carstairs pleaded out and Kit served thirty days and was given a few months' probation.

"Duane Carstairs," she said to herself. "The name means nothing to me now but tell me a little more."

Homes filled her in about both Duane and Wendy and the unsolved murder.

"Audrey, I retired from the force a couple of years ago and I'm doing detective work with my partner, Jack Novak. We're part of a squad that's trying to solve Wendy Carstairs's murder. We've talked to lots of people and we're still in the dark. Your name came up on a long list that had some connection with the Carstairs."

"Yeah, I'm beginning to recall a little of that whole thing," she said. "Carstairs was just another trick to me. He had a lot of money and a nice apartment downtown and one out here in Roswell. He didn't expect much from me, paid me a bundle and never hurt me so I saw him several times. Nothing happened out of the ordinary that I can remember."

"Now that I think of it, I met the wife once. Yeah, Wendy. She came home one night when her husband and I were finishing up. Didn't seem to bother her at all. I remember now that she asked me if I'd stay for a threesome. I wasn't into that so I told her I had another date. She was pretty. That's about all I can come up with. Oh, and her husband? He gave me some dope when he paid me. They were both using. Not too smart but he seemed like an okay guy."

"Well, that helps. I sure appreciate you seeing me, Audrey. Here's my card in case you think of anything else that might be useful to us. We've really got nothing to go on."

Audrey was deep in thought. "Come to think of it, Homes, here's something you can try. You might remember Amber Still. She called herself Dyno Mite on the street. Amber's the one that told me about Duane Carstairs. She used to see him pretty regularly. She had something going with the wife – Wendy – too. She might be helpful. We've stayed in touch over the years. Last time I saw her she was in those apartments over on Crawford – the ones with the playground you can see from the street. She's been down a lot and I help her out sometimes."

"I know the place. Thanks for the tip. I'll head over there now. Take care of yourself."

"Homes, take it easy with her. She's had it pretty rough the last few years. I think she's been doing okay recently but she relapses every once in a while, so she's still using. Don't give her any grief."

They both stood up.

"It was great to see you, Homes. You were always straight with me and tried to help. I never forgot that. If I come up with anything I'll give you a call."

They hugged briefly and Homes left the apartment and walked to his car.

8

He made a quick stop at Roswell PD to look up any info about Dyno Mite/Amber Still. Other than her long arrest sheet there were no other significant details. Her last arrest had been about three months ago.

He spotted the playground outside the apartments Audrey had mentioned and pulled into the parking area. The place was pretty run down, cans and other litter lying around. The buildings could have used some work too. Paint would have helped but some areas needed major repairs. He found Amber's building and walked up the two flights to her third-floor apartment and knocked. There was no sound at first and then he heard some movement toward the door.

If Amber was close to Audrey's age – about forty – she looked all of sixty. Time, her occupation and hard drugs had not been kind to her. Homes had seen a lot of this when he was still on the force but it always depressed him.

"Yeah, what do you want," Amber said. She looked him over for a minute. "I smell cop."

"I guess that smell never leaves. My name is Homes Kinney and I was on the Roswell force for over twenty years. I'd like to ask you a few questions about an unsolved murder." He explained the details of the Carstairs case and some of the people they had been interviewing. He didn't mention Audrey's name, thinking that might affect the two women's friendship.

"I didn't commit no murder, mister," she said, "but I guess you can come in."

They sat down in the kitchenette. There were dishes in the sink and the drab room needed a good cleaning.

"I'd offer you a drink but I don't have nothin,' she said. The odor of alcohol from her was unmistakable. She lit up a cigarette. "I think you might have arrested me once back in the day," she said. "I went by Dyno Mite back then."

Homes nodded. "It's possible. You do look familiar. You haven't changed much," he lied. "I know it's been a long time. Can you remember anything about the Carstairs, especially around the time of the murder?"

She thought a minute, drew on her cigarette. "Is there anything in this for me?"

"I can give you a little but you have to be straight with me," Homes said.

"Sure. Yeah, I knew the Carstairs pretty well. I had – uh – dates with the husband. Was his name Don or David?"

"Duane."

"Right. Duane. He was maybe short and chubby, Losing his hair. Drank a lot. Did some drugs. Always generous with the white stuff. It didn't take long for me to get him off, I remember that. His wife –" She looked at the ceiling, trying to remember.

"Wendy," Homes said.

"Yeah, Wendy. We got together a few times, too. Great body on that woman. She was always good for a laugh and a few bucks. Even some dope. She's the one that started me shootin' up the hard stuff. She loved it." Suddenly her voice changed. "So did I."

"That's what I've been hearing. Did you ever overhear anything about his business or any personal stuff they might have talked about? I'm looking for names, mostly."

"Sure. The guy talked a lot about his business, trying to impress me. But he really wasn't that smart. I knew he had a lot of cash and I didn't give a damn about his business. I did get the feeling that drugs were a part of what he was into. I remember he mentioned Mexico a lot. The wife didn't say much. She was there for the good times and I gave her what she liked. They argued once or twice but they were too high to make sense out of it. They were both big tippers. Is any of this helping?"

Homes nodded. "You're doing fine. You have a good memory. Anything else?"

Amber rubbed her face and looked around the kitchen. "Wish I had a drink. Maybe there was another women showed up once or twice. Another good looker. She might have been in show business or somethin.' She and Wendy were tight. I wouldn't have minded makin' it with her but she wasn't interested. That's about it."

"That was a big help," Homes said, not meaning it. He hadn't even taken a note but would type up the interview when he got back in the office. "Here's my card. Give me a call if you think of something else." He gave her a twenty-dollar bill along with the card.

"Thanks a lot, mister," she said. She looked him over again. "If there's anything else I can do for you just let me know." Her attempt at a smile failed and was more of a frown.

"I'll do that," Homes said, standing up. "Take care of yourself."

He let himself out of the apartment.

◆ ◆ ◆

"I appreciate you seeing me, Booster."

Jack walked along Booster Desmond's photo gallery covering one wall of his uptown Atlanta apartment. "I was at the stadium when you made this wicked basket. Man, what a shot."

"Yeah, that was a good night," Booster said. "I was sober, off the weed and feeling fine. After that, the crowd always shouted *BOOST IT BOOST IT* whenever I hit the floor. The name stuck." They walked into the living room. "My man Rudy told me you'd be callin.' Now what's all this shit about Wendy Carstairs' murder? Man, that was so long ago . . . " His voice drifted off as he filled a water glass with Courvoisier and took a sip. "You sure I can't get you anything?"

"No, Boost. Thanks just the same." Jack sat down across from him.

"Rudy told me you give up the hard stuff. Don't know what I'd do without it now," he said, smiling. "What you want to know?"

"Anything you can tell me about the Carstairs – Wendy and Duane. Anything you can remember."

"Mmmmm . . . Don't know nothin' about that husband but I could talk all night about that redheaded bitch." Booster laughed out loud and clapped his hands. "She couldn't get enough of the Boost, I can tell you that. One fine lookin' woman. Only trouble with her was she kept me drinkin' too much and bumpin' up. Can't do that and play pro ball. Not for long."

"Bumpin' up? Tell me about that," Jack said.

"Man, you a cop and you ain't heard a that?" Booster laughed. "Bumpin' up means smokin' or shootin' cocaine and ecstasy. That's a fine high, man, while it lasts. It makes sex all the better, know what I mean?"

"I get it now. Did she – did Wendy ever talk business – about the business her husband was in?"

"Only business she was interested in was Booster business," he said, laughing. "Rudy say he was her main man but I had him beat. She used to beg me for more. Yes sir, them were the days."

"And you never had much to do with the husband?"

"Not at all. Oh, he was around from time to time. Used to like to watch us doin' it, you know? At first I didn't mind but it started buggin' me after a while so I shut him down. He never seemed smart enough to be a big executive."

"Ever meet any of their friends?"

"Lemme think," Booster said. "Only one I can recall was that singer – what the hell was her name -?"

"Alice. Alice Townsend."

"That's the one. She was buzzin' around me and Wendy lots at times. We invited her into our little circle you might say" – Booster laughed hard again – "but she never joined us. Man I used to dream about havin' both of them at once. You ever hear her sing?"

"Only on her albums," Jack said. "So nobody talked about business?"

"I tole you, man. We was too busy getting' it on. I never gave a shit about her husband's business. Neither did she as far as I could tell. I knew he was pullin' in the big money, but not as much as me."

"Any guesses as to who might have killed her?"

"It sure as shit wasn't me, man, I can tell you that. Hope you find the cat that did it, though. Didn't he take her head off?"

"Yeah. Pretty gruesome."

"You got that right. Hey, you want an autograph or anything?"

Jack smiled and stood up. "I'd love one, Boost, if you don't mind."

Booster opened a drawer in a table. "How about one on that photo you like so much?" He scribbled something on the picture and handed it to Jack. They shook hands.

"Thanks a lot for your time, Boost. I miss seeing you out there on the court."

"Nice of you to say, man. They been talkin' to me about coachin' but I don't know about that shit. The money would be good but I still got enough to get by." He laughed loudly again.

The two men walked to the door and Jack handed Booster his card. "If you think of anything that might help," he said.

"Will do. Stay cool, Jack."

9

Jack and Homes were doing what had become a daily evaluation of their interviews and a check on their progress.

"We've just about cleared these interviews," Homes said. "What do you think?"

Jack tossed a file on the table between them. "I still think most of them are lying. They're telling us the very same things, almost as if they rehearsed them. There's something going on behind the scenes that's shutting us out."

"I'd have to agree with you, Jack. Now, what do we do about it?"

"The only thing I know to do is to push harder on the key witnesses – the ones that spent the most time with the Carstairs, whether in their business or in some more personal capacity."

"You mean like sex"

"That's exactly what I mean. If there's any chance to solve this murder, we stick to two things. We follow the money and we follow the sex. I'm going to start by going back to Alice Townsend. She's singing at her club tonight and we're going to meet afterwards."

Homes smiled. "I assume you are mixing work and play with this one."

"Not really," Jack said. "Homes, has it ever seemed suspicious or unusual to you that a blues singer past her prime was able to buy her own nightclub right after the Wendy Carstairs murder? The club still operates and even books some pretty big names like Tony Bennett."

"I see what you're getting at but I never really thought about it."

"I checked the real estate records when the sale occurred just a few months after Wendy was murdered. Alice paid almost two million for the place. In cash. Since when does a local blues singer who has never made big bucks come up with that kind of money? And guess who she bought it from?"

"You telling me the Carstairs owned the place?"

"In a way. The club, which had never made a profit, was owned by an outfit called Sounds A Million. Turns out it was one of the Breckenridge's holding companies, owned by Duane Carstairs. There's more. Alice's apartment is furnished with high-priced furniture and original artwork that's even more expensive. It's been twenty years since she bought the club but the money apparently keeps rolling in from somewhere."

"Sounds like you're on to something, buddy. What do you want me to focus on now?"

"Finish up the last couple of interviews. Then go back and talk to those two women that had relationships with Duane and Wendy Carstairs. I have the feeling they both know more than they're telling us."

◆ ◆ ◆

"You were in fine voice tonight," Jack said as he and Alice walked to his car.

"Thanks. *I Can't Get Started With You* is one of my favorite tunes," she said.

"Who wrote that? Gershwin?"

"That's right. The version I like best isn't even a vocal. It's by a horn player from the 30s named Bunny Berigan."

"I'm not familiar with him. My favorite would be by Sinatra."

"Everybody's favorite something is by Sinatra," she said, smiling.

They were silent driving the short distance to her apartment.

"You feelin' okay?' she asked.

"I'm fine," Jack said. "I do want to talk to you about a few things."

"Business before pleasure? I'm disappointed," she said as they walked into her place.

She turned into his arms and they embraced slowly for a while. "You can always change your mind," she said.

"It's important."

"Okay. Let's go into the living room."

Instead of sitting beside her on the sofa Jack pulled up a chair across from her.

"Alice, we've been going over some old business records of yours and I have a few questions."

Alice poured herself a drink and sat down. "Sure. Fire away."

Jack decided to get right to the point. "You purchased the Dorset club about twenty years ago for cash but your bank and savings accounts didn't have nearly that much in them. Can you explain that?"

Alice had no reaction. "Why should I have to? It has nothing to do with the murder you're investigating. A good friend loaned me the money. Anything wrong with that?"

"Not at all. Do you mind telling me who that was?"

"You wouldn't know him. Or her." Alice took another sip of her drink.

Jack watched her for a moment. "About your club . . . The FBI has examined the tax returns for the last ten years. It doesn't seem to be making much money. In fact, you've shown losses for all of those years. Yet you seem to be living well and can afford some pretty expensive toys. Any explanation?"

"No. I'm sure my accountants can answer your questions about tax returns. I was told this would be a good investment as a tax loss. Jack, will you please tell me what this has to do with Wendy Carstairs' murder?"

"The team doing the investigating – and that includes the FBI's forensics division – thinks there may be a connection between you, the Carstairs and the Breckenridge Company that was formed and headed by Duane Carstairs before his death. You are one of several people who are being investigated." Jack paused and decided to go for it. "See, we found this old diary of Wendy's. She writes a lot about you and Duane and Breckenridge, so we know plenty about what was going on and who was doing what."

"I see." Alice stood up. "Jack, I think you'd better leave. I thought we were on the way to forming a very nice relationship and I see I was wrong. I don't like being – used like this. If you need any further information you can contact my attorneys. Oh, and Jack, I like you; you're a nice guy. Don't get yourself into a shitload of trouble for no reason over something that happened years ago. You can let yourself out." She walked out of the room.

10

❝ Homes, I don't mind seeing you again but I thought we were finished the other day." Audrey Taylor was not smiling but appeared to be unruffled by Homes' questions.

"Sorry, Audrey. Some other things have come up and I'm going back over a few of the witnesses we've already talked to. When you were seeing Duane Carstairs in the old days did you ever meet a friend of his wife's named Alice?"

Audrey put down her coffee cup very carefully, as if in deep thought. "Let me think. Alice Townsend? No. No, I don't recall anyone by that name. Why do you ask?"

Homes had not mentioned Alice's last name but Audrey had used it right away.

"She was a fairly well-known nightclub singer at the time. Still has a place in the city. She and Wendy Carstairs were close friends. I thought you might have met her and overheard anything that might help us with the investigation."

"Nothing comes to mind, Homes. I'm sure I would have remembered something like that. Any other questions?" She stood up.

Homes stayed seated. "No, not really. Oh, there is one thing I wanted to mention. Audrey, we found this diary of Wendy Carstairs and that has tipped us off to a lot of stuff that was going on in Breckenridge and the people that were involved. Your name has come up several times."

Audrey was very well-controlled but Homes could tell he had bothered her with that one. She took her time, then - "No. I've tried to recall everything that might help." She started walking away. "I really need to get to work."

Homes had checked and her shift at the rehab center didn't start for another three hours.

"Sure," he said, standing up. "Sorry to bother you. It was good to see you again."

"You, too."

They both walked to the door.

"Homes, retirement is supposed to help you relax," Audrey said. "You should take it easy. Maybe this old case is bringing up bad memories."

"They usually do," Homes said. "Thanks again for your help."

◆ ◆ ◆

Back in their office, Homes and Jack talked over their recent interviews.

"Did it sound like a warning?" Homes asked him.

"That's what it sounded like to me," Jack said. "It was vague and she didn't sound angry when she said it. But I took it as a warning. You say you may have gotten the same thing from Audrey Taylor?"

"Maybe. The main thing was when she used Alice Townsend's last name when I hadn't mentioned it at all. She did it without thinking and that got my attention. Then she told me she had to be at work when she wasn't scheduled for three hours. Finally she said that I ought to relax in my retirement. Maybe it was nothing but it set off red lights for me. Another thing that bugged me was that the Breckenridge COO, Maxine Turner, said Duane Carstairs was a genius. But everyone else I talked to said he was pretty dumb. Oh, and I used the diary thing a couple of times and thought I got some good reactions."

Jack smiled at his friend. "Good for you. Come to think of it, that's what Booster Desmond said about Duane and so did Alice. Homes, you and I have been doing this kind of work for a long time. More than twenty years for you. We're sensitive to slips by witnesses who may be covering up." He thought for a moment. "We may be on to something. I need to check in with Bob Sheppard today to see if the FBI has anything new. Then let's talk some more."

◆ ◆ ◆

"Jack, it's Diane." He recognized Homes' girlfriend's voice immediately. "Homes has been shot. I'm at Northside Hospital now. Get over here as fast as you can."

"Is he okay?"

"He's in the ER now. The docs are working on him."

It took only ten minutes for Jack to get to the hospital, breaking speed limits all the way. Diane was waiting for him at the entrance.

"How – "

"He'll be okay," she said. "The shot grazed his head. He lost some blood but there was no brain damage. We can't see him right now." They sat down in the waiting area.

"Any more details?" Jack asked.

"Not so far. I called this into Bob Sheppard downtown so the FBI is alerted."

"Jesus. What was he doing? Where was he?"

"He was coming out of the Roswell mall and walking to his car. It was late. There weren't many cars or people around. Thank God the shot attracted some attention and the police were called. He wasn't conscious then so they haven't been able to question him. The doc says we can probably see him tomorrow. We should call after ten." She stopped and cleared her throat. "I don't know what's the matter with me. I should be crying or something."

"It'll hit later," he said. "When you can see him and talk to him. We both may be crying then."

◆ ◆ ◆

The first thing Homes saw was Jack and Diane standing beside his hospital bed looking anxious.

"Since neither one of you is a priest, I must still be alive," he said. "What the hell happened?"

Jack and Diane brought him up to date, as the nurse came in, checked his temperature and blood pressure, and left.

"I don't remember a damn thing after I walked out of the mall," Homes said. He looked at Jack. "This is a real switch, buddy. Me in the hospital and you standing next to my bed. And you're even sober. That's got to be a first. Especially since the beautiful woman with you is my girlfriend."

"How are you really feeling?" Diane asked.

"Hell of a headache but otherwise okay. Must have scratched my leg when I fell at the mall. Jack, I'm thinking this cold case of ours is getting warmer."

"I think it just boiled over," Jack said. "Roswell PD has been checking in all day to see if you're still alive. I'll tell the next one who calls that you say you are but we can't tell any difference."

"Ha," Homes grunted. "When can I get out of here?"

"They're still checking x-rays. I think maybe in a day or two," Diane said.

"Yeah, the first x-rays of your head showed there was nothing there," Jack said.

"Old, old Joke, buddy. I know you can do better than that. What do we do next?"

"More of the same. Now the Atlanta and Roswell police are involved big time, to say nothing of the FBI," Jack said.

"That reminds me; I have to get back to work," Diane said. "Sheppard said I am too personally involved but I told him it wasn't that personal."

They all laughed.

"Jack, tell me she's kidding," Homes said.

"I'll let her show you later. I have a few things to do so I'll leave you for a while. I'll be in touch. Diane, some agents are posted outside. The fun is over. This thing has gotten very real, very quickly." He headed for the door.

"Jack," Homes called out.

"Yeah."

"Start wearing your gun."

"Got it on me," Jack said, slapping his left arm pit.

11

"So he's doing better?" FBI district supervisor Bob Sheppard and agent Diane Nguyen were talking to Jack about Homes.

"Well, he's complaining a lot," Jack said, smiling. "Another day or two and he'll be home. I don't know how we're going to keep him from jumping right back into things, though. Maybe Diane can help."

"You know as well as I that no one can slow him down," she said.

"So what's new with you Feds on our murder investigation?" Jack asked.

Sheppard tossed a red file with large blue FBI letters embossed on the cover across the table to Jack. "Take a look at this," he said.

A large 8 X 10 photo stared up at him as he opened the file.

"Yeah, this is a photo of Duane Carstairs. We've got a similar one in the old Roswell PD file in the office."

Sheppard grimaced. "What if I told you it isn't him?"

Jack looked at it again. "Nope, that's him alright."

"No it's not, Jack. It's his brother, Donald." Sheppard glanced at Diane and shook his head.

"Where the hell did he come from?" Jack said. "There's no record of him in any file I've read or in any conversation I've had with a half-dozen witnesses. Duane's business bio doesn't mention any brother. In fact it says he has no living relatives."

"That's what we thought," Sheppard said. "This photo and information just turned up from one of our agents in Colorado. This guy Donald has lived out there for years under another name. Calls himself Arnold Folkman. New DNA tracing found him. They analyzed some hair follicles from Duane

Carstairs and ran them against possible relatives in a huge nation-wide database. That's standard procedure in these cold cases. So this Folkman guy was a hit. More than a hit; his DNA was a dead-on match for Duane Carstairs. To be certain we pulled up Duane's DNA and it was an identical match with Folkman."

"Folkman – or whoever he is - had an old arrest for some minor drug use and Colorado requires a blood sample in those cases. That's how they got his DNA in their database, along with his prints. When they pulled up his record we got this photo. My guy in Colorado had the Carstairs file and remembered Duane's photo and saw the similarity. But there's a lot more to the story."

"Lay it on me."

"First, to be certain these two names were the same guy we traced all the way back to Duane Carstairs' birth announcement. Sure enough, his mother gave birth to identical twins, Duane and Donald. Then we found the Arnold Folkman name all over legal papers in our old Breckenridge files. We had never paid any attention to it before. From what we've been able to determine so far, Donald Carstairs was the real brains behind Duane's company, using the Folkman name. In fact, we think he still is."

"He what?" Jack stood up, pushed his chair back, and threw the file on the desk. "You mean these two guys are identical twins and this Folkman guy has actually been running the company all along?"

"I mean more than that, Jack. This gets complicated and maybe Diane can explain it better than I, but these two are or were identical in every way, down to their DNA."

Jack shook his head. "That's impossible. DNA is like fingerprints. No two are alike. Every human being's DNA is different from every other person."

"Not exactly, Jack" Diane said. "The science of this is pretty thick and I'm not sure I understand it all myself. As good as our DNA science is, our labs can't differentiate in every single way between DNA from truly identical twins. That's what these two guys are. There was a German rape case about ten years ago that brought this all to light. I think they're still arguing over it.

Last I heard, the German defense team is still trying to get a dismissal because the lab was comparing DNA from semen with DNA from saliva. Apparently there's a big difference. There's no test in the United States that can distinguish some forms of DNA from genuine identical twins. So there's no solid law on this subject, at least not in the good old USA."

"So what? Even if this is true, what difference does it make in our case? What do we care if these guys have the same DNA or not?"

Sheppard and Diane looked at each other. "Jack, you've read the lab report on Wendy Carstairs' body?"

"Read it? I've practically got it memorized."

Diane nodded. "So you remember that we found a fair amount of DNA."

"Yeah." Jack was becoming upset. He could see this case falling apart for some weird science reason and he wanted to break it apart.

"We know there were two male DNA samples in or on Wendy and we've identified them as Duane and Rudy Simmons. The female hairs belong to Alice Townsend. What if Donald Carstairs murdered Wendy and not Duane, as we've always thought? What if it's true that he's still running the Breckenridge Corporation and their business involves drug dealing and arms shipments, as we suspect, and probably a lot more? How the hell can we prove it's him – Donald – and not Duane? A good defense lawyer could bring up this wacky German case and claim Donald wasn't involved at all, in anything. He could get away with everything from guns and drugs to murder."

"Holy shit," Jack said.

The three of them sat silently and stared at each other.

"Now that we're playing *what if,* here's something else to worry about," Jack said.

"What's that?" Sheppard asked.

"What if neither of them murdered her? What if Alice Townsend did it? Or our sports suspects, Rudy Simmons and Booster Desmond? Oh, what the hell. What if it's someone we haven't even identified yet! Wait till I tell Homes about this one."

◆ ◆ ◆

"I was going to cook dinner for you the other night," Alice said. "And you could have had anything you wanted for dessert."

"I'm sorry I missed that," Jack said, "especially the dessert. Thanks."

"It was your own fault. I see you're carrying a gun."

"Goes with the job. And after Homes got shot I thought it would be a good idea."

"Have you ever shot someone?" Alice said.

"Several someones. It's never pleasant but sometimes necessary. You have nothing to worry about," he said, smiling.

"I wasn't worried. I was going to say it was a smart move."

"Alice, tell me about Donald Carstairs or should I say Arnold Folkman?" He was trying to catch her off guard and it worked.

She stared at him for a long time. "Jack, this is a lot bigger than you know. And a lot more dangerous. Too many people are involved. People in high places. They can pull a lot of strings to protect their interests. And one of those strings is murder. What was it they said about the banks after our monetary system failed a few years ago? They were too big to fail? That's what this is all about. Breckenridge is too big to be exposed. There are billions of dollars at stake here, Jack. And people's lives. People like you and others close to you."

"Alice, I didn't expect to get involved with you as deeply as I have. I want to help you now. There are lots of ways for you to cooperate with us and protect yourself."

She chuckled, got up from the sofa and poured herself a very large brandy.

"I thought for a while we could work things out, too. I knew you weren't stupid. The trouble is that this – thing – Breckenridge has had going on for so long is very complicated." She looked around her apartment. "This is my life, Jack. This is what I want. And need. I can't afford to give it up, in the truest sense of that term . I'd appreciate it if you'd leave now. And, for your own good, don't come back."

"Alice, I mentioned before that we know a great deal about the Breckenridge operation from Wendy's diary. I'm guessing your part in it involved laundering money for them through your club. It's only a question of time before it all comes out. I can take care of myself. It's you I'm worried about. Alice, the FBI will be here sooner or later."

Alice grimaced as she stood up with Jack and they walked toward each other.

"I want you to remember what you're missing," she said, putting her arms around him.

12

Jack was driving on the I-285 loop around Atlanta when the black SUV pulled up alongside him and held its position. He glanced over to see the driver and passenger both wearing ski masks. The passenger side window was down and a man was pointing a very large .45 at him. Jack hit his brakes hard and swerved just as the shot rang out and shattered his window. He slowed to a stop alongside the road and took a deep breath, then dialed 911.

◆ ◆ ◆

Diane was putting some antiseptic on the small scratches on Jack's face while Homes looked on anxiously.

"Jack, I've got to say that this is carrying our togetherness way too far. First they take a shot at me; now you. You sure you don't have any more cuts?"

"Nope. This is it. Thanks for the repair job, Diane. I think this means we all have to be even more careful than we have been.

"Here's an idea," Diane said. "Let's use an old FBI technique. If we have to go out anywhere let's go in twos. It'll just make us more aware of anything or anyone approaching us that just looks wrong. And an extra gun won't hurt, either."

"That's a damn good idea, Diane," Jack said. "Roswell PD has offered to station a couple of guys outside our place but I turned them down for the time being."

"So what do we do now?" Homes said.

Jack thought a minute. "Homes, when you were investigating the Berkshire Corporation twenty years ago was there any employee you talked to who you felt was being straight up with you – someone you believed you could trust? My idea needs a person who is still working there now."

Homes pulled out his Berkshire file and flipped through a couple of pages. "Yeah, this guy – Robert Sawyer – was pretty straightforward as far as I could tell. He's still on the current witness list, too. Why?"

"We still need to break something loose and I'll be damned if I'm going to sit around and wait for one of us to be shot again. Homes, why don't you and Diane interview this Sawyer guy and see if he knows anything about Arnold Folkman or Donald Carstairs or what's been going on at Breckenridge. He's worked there for twenty years so he must have seen or heard something that can help us. Do you remember what he does?"

"Not really," Homes said. "He was a younger guy and more than somebody who got coffee for the executives. I remember he was hired to get their new computer system up and running. Seemed pretty sharp."

"Good. He may have loosened up after all this time and have something he wants to talk about. See if you can set up a time to talk to him, preferably outside the office."

"Will do. What's on your agenda?"

"Keeping our two-person rule in mind, I'll stay here and go over our files and work the phones. Call me if you two get anything. Diane, do you have any suggestions?"

"No, I think we're doing everything that makes sense. Let's get moving."

13

"So, Mr. Sawyer, thanks for agreeing to meet with us privately," Homes said. "The things we'll be discussing are extremely confidential. We appreciate your cooperation. I've explained on the phone that we're investigating Wendy Carstairs's murder. We've also found some suspicious information about Breckenridge and that's why I asked for your assistance."

"Glad to help. I always liked Mr. Carstairs and his wife. Their deaths – or murders – still bother a lot of us at Breckenridge. And please call me Robert."

"Sure, Robert. I'm Homes and this is agent Diane Nguyen with the FBI. I actually remember talking to you twenty years ago. I think you had just started at Breckenridge."

"That's right. I was twenty-two years old and was hired to update and modernize their computer system. I remember you, too."

Homes smiled. "I'll be honest with you. We're interested in information in two areas. Most importantly, we're trying to solve the murder of Wendy Carstairs and certainly the possibility that her husband was also murdered. Next, we've always suspected that the company was involved in some businesses that were not exactly legal, to put it mildly. Can you tell us anything that might help resolve either of those two investigations?"

Sawyer thought for a moment and pulled out a large file he had brought with him. "You told me a little about your investigation when we talked on the phone and I have some material with me to refresh my mind. I can only give you gossip about who might have killed Mrs. Carstairs. We all suspected either her husband or the baseball player she was seeing. I sensed that both of them were jealous about the other and their relationships with Mrs. Carstairs. I really don't have any hard evidence. I was always loyal to Mr. Carstairs despite the fact that I never thought he was that smart. He gave me free reign of the computer department, paid me well and promoted me often. I cannot say the same for our present COO, Ms. Turner – Maxine Turner. She is never cordial and gives the impression that she really does not know much about what the company is involved in."

Diane nodded. "And exactly what is the company involved in, Robert?"

"I'd like to give you a direct answer to that but the fact is that Breckenridge has so many hidden corporations, holding companies, and foreign bank accounts that this would be hard to do. And while my position at Breckenridge is Director of Computer systems, it came to my attention several years ago that there is another elaborate company computer system located somewhere in Colorado. So I'm not certain how much of my own information is valid. I can tell you what I suspect."

"Please do," Diane said.

"There's never been any question in my mind that the company has been dealing in drugs and illegal gun sales for the last twenty years. Both are booming businesses, of course, and continue to grow. There are people – I'll call them a crew – who work outside the company in the area of drugs. I don't know names. I do think that one of the main drug distributors in the Atlanta area is being paid by Breckenridge and lives somewhere close by. I suspect that gun sales are handled directly by a senior executive unknown to me."

"Anything else?"

"I'm able to look at the financial records of course, but even there things have been covered up masterfully by a financial specialty firm in Colorado. For instance, drug purchases and payoffs are referred to as computer purchases and equipment. Since this is my area I can tell you that I have not seen many of these computers or upgrades. When I ask Ms. Turner about them she tells me that Breckenridge has many subsidiary offices throughout the country and most of the new computers are sent to those areas. However, I happen to know that there are no other Breckenridge offices anywhere, just those hidden corporations using other names."

"Interesting," Diane said. "What about the bank accounts?"

"As far as I can tell they are all offshore. The main account is in Switzerland. All the accounts are held in the names of subsidiaries. We are even paid through one of these other companies. That's as much as I know."

"Robert, have you ever heard of or seen the name of an Arnold Folkman?" Homes had been making notes while Sawyer was talking.

"Now that's interesting. Over the past twenty years his name has occurred in our records many times. He has no title that I've ever seen but he receives a substantial amount of money from the company through the offshore accounts. His travel record is also extensive, including many trips to France, primarily to that country's possession in the Caribbean, St. Barthelemy. In my opinion, the destinations listed on his travel vouchers could very well indicate that he is the senior executive I mentioned before who is involved in both drugs and gun sales. In my twenty years with the company I have never seen the man, although I have seen correspondence sent to him in Colorado."

Homes and Diane glanced at each other. "Let me run a few other names by you. How about Alice Townsend?"

Sawyer nodded and smiled. "Yes, I happen to be a huge fan of Ms. Townsend's work and I make it a point to hear her sing whenever she appears at the Dorset Club. Interestingly, Breckenridge uses the club for very private events called training sessions for which we pay substantial amounts to Ms. Townsend on a regular basis. I have to say that during my twenty years here I have never heard of any employee attending one of these sessions, nor have I ever been asked to participate myself. It's obvious that the club is used for an entirely different purpose."

"What about a Rudy Simmons?"

"Of course I know Mr. Simmons from his playing days with the Braves here in Atlanta. He is also paid substantial amounts periodically through one of the private bank accounts and he is listed in our files as *Entertainment*. I saw Mr. Simmons frequently at Breckenridge when I first joined the company. He and Mrs. Carstairs were – uh – friendly. I have not seen him regularly in the building in quite a few years. I must say that when he was seeing Mrs. Carstairs they had quite a few arguments which were heard by many employees."

Homes continued to take notes. "Just for the hell of it, what about Audrey Taylor?"

"Oh, yes," Sawyer agreed. "That is yet another name that appears regularly on our financial payouts in rather large sums under the account name *Business*."

"Is that it?"

"Yes, that's all. Oh, I've never met this Audrey person but I know she lives in the Roswell area. I also suspect from the large financial payouts made to her that she may well be involved in the drug distribution system at a high level."

"Diane, do you have anything else?"

"No, I think Mr. Sawyer – Robert – has been very helpful. Robert, I think Homes mentioned this to you on the phone but let me reinforce it. This is a highly confidential investigation and you should keep all knowledge of our conversation private in every respect. I will also tell you that I'm sure the Atlanta FBI office will be investigating Breckenridge very soon and subpoenaing all computer records. I hope you will be as cooperative with them as you've been with us."

"You can be certain I will do so. I must admit that I have been troubled all these years suspecting that Breckenridge was involved in illegal activities. But, as I said, I am paid well and left alone to run my end of the business so I never said anything. That's not an excuse; I regret not having spoken out about all of this before now."

14

Jack and Homes were back in their office going over Homes' notes from the meeting with Robert Sawyer. Bob Sheppard had called Diane back to the downtown FBI office after reading her report from the visit to Breckenridge.

"Man, this sounds like you two hit the jackpot," Jack said.

"Yes, and I think we've only scratched the surface," Homes said. "Diane is suggesting to Sheppard that he get the appropriate subpoenas and pay a visit to Breckenridge as soon as possible. I think they deserve an FBI raid. Diane says they prefer the term *private incursion.*"

"Too bad you didn't get any real tips about Wendy Carstairs' murder," Jack said. "But I think we may pick up some helpful clues when the FBI does their thing."

Jack's cell phone interrupted their meeting.

"Jack, I need to see you and Homes. It's urgent." It was Bob Sheppard at the FBI.

"Sure, Bob. We can be downtown in about a half-hour, traffic permitting."

"What do you think's on Sheppard's mind?" Homes said to Jack as they zigzagged through traffic on 400 headed south into Atlanta.

"No idea. He may want to know if I've remembered any more about those assholes who shot at me but I gave all I had to him as well as to Roswell PD."

They pulled into the FBI parking lot on Century Parkway, secured their weapons in their trunk, set the car alarm, and entered the building. It was one flight up to Sheppard's office. Sheppard and Diane were both seated around the long conference table, looking gloomy.

"What's up?" Jack said.

"Jack, this is hard to say. We're going to drop the case."

"What case? You mean –"

"Yes, the Wendy Carstairs murder."

"Wait a minute," Homes said. "Jack and I were almost killed chasing down shit about this case. You can't quit now."

"It's out of my hands, Homes. Believe me, I'm sorry."

"Sorry doesn't cut it," Homes said. "Diane, are you in on this, too?"

She looked at Sheppard. "Homes, this decision was made way above our heads. This comes from the top, in DC."

Jack stood up. "Bob, I think I need to remind you that what started out to be an investigation of an old cold murder has become a red-hot attempted murder case involving my partner Homes and me. It's a matter of record with the Roswell Police Department and the Georgia Highway Patrol where the attempts occurred. The decision from your DC office has nothing to do with that and has no authority over it. We intend to continue our investigation no matter what you do."

The two men left the office and drove hurriedly back to Roswell.

15

The knock on their office door the next day interrupted Jack and Homes. They both checked the security monitor and were surprised to see Diane outside. Homes got up to let her in. "Nice to see you, babe, but I thought you were off the case."

She hugged Homes and waved to Jack. "I've taken some personal leave to see if there is anything I can do to help," she said, sitting down at their conference table. "Bob wants you to know that he's with you, too, and, off the record, will send you any information he gets. He's also in touch with Washington trying to find out who pulled the plug on this case."

"That's good to know," Jack said. "After what we've been through on other investigations, a friend like Sheppard will come in handy. He surprised me when he said his office was dropping the case, Diane. But I figured he might find some way to stay in touch. I also made a couple of contacts with your folks in Washington when we were handling the Nashville murders case last year. I'll be calling them soon to see what the hell's going on up there. I'm glad you're here for another reason. Homes and I think you should move in with us for your own protection. As you know, the apartment half of this place has plenty of room, including an extra bedroom."

"She won't be needing that," Homes interrupted.

Jack and Diane smiled. "We also have a lot of early warning gadgets set up outside and in, and enough firepower of our own. The people taking shots at me and Homes are obviously wealthy and powerful. I'm sure they know a lot about us, our friends and our routines. You'll be better off here than in your own apartment."

Homes smiled. "Gee, I wonder if I'd really like to have my girlfriend here all the time running around in her PJs."

Diane made a face at him. "I'm glad you haven't lost your sense of humor, buddy. But I have to say that with half your head shaved, you're really not that attractive. You have more of a Hannibal Lecter look. I'd be happy to move in with you two bozos. Oh, and I brought my own weapon," she said, slapping the holstered .40 caliber Glock at her waist.

"I'm glad both of you can find some humor in this situation. Diane, it's great to have you with us. Now let's get down to figuring out an action plan for where we go from here."

"And where DO we go, detective?" Homes said.

"Maybe this will help," Diane said. "Bob handed it to me when I left the office. You know how we try to keep track of our most wanted guys, especially if they're known to be in our area? Take a look at this." She handed both men a sheet of paper with the FBI logo embossed on top. There were five names on the sheet with a brief bio after each name.

"Hit men?" Homes said. "You mean . . ."

"We don't know if any of these guys are the ones that tried to take out you and Jack. All we know is that some of them are in the area and it's a good bet they were involved," Diane said. "The problem is in finding them."

"Homes, don't you know someone –"

Homes interrupted his friend. "Yeah, Tony Corona was my best CI when Roswell would occasionally loan me to Atlanta PD. He was in tight with the mob for a long time when they were running things downtown. He may still be. If anyone knows where these guys are it's him."

"So how do we find this Corona?" Diane said.

"I know where he used to hang out. That's where we start. Jack and I will take this one, Diane. Do what you can on the phones from here. If we get in trouble we'll yell. And by the way, I know from experience you can handle the tough stuff. You've saved my ass a couple of times already. You'll get your turn, I promise."

16

"This is your call, Homes," Jack said as they headed downtown. "It's been a while since you and Tony were in touch."

"Yeah, but my guys in Atlanta PD say he's still alive and well. Remember Bill Corral? I called him before we left and he gave me Tony's address and the names of three places he's liable to hang out. First one is The Inferno."

"Really?" Jack said. "That's been an Italian mob hangout since the old days."

"Some things never change, Jack. When the Blacks came into power in Atlanta the old mob families had learned from the past. Instead of declaring war they sat down with the new guys and decided they could both do better by dividing up the territories and keeping the peace. The Inferno is still a major hangout for Italians."

"But we can't just go busting in there and grab Tony in front of his buddies. They'll know we're cops or at least that we used to be. We could get him in a lot of trouble."

"Right. So if he's there we'll just talk to him for a minute, along with a few other guys, and then leave. I'll slip him a note with my cell number. And if he's not there, I've got his last known address and two other Italian hangouts to check."

The two men parked outside The Inferno which didn't appear to be too busy. They walked inside, looked around, and went up to the bar.

"Hi," Homes said. "We're looking for Tony Corona."

"Never heard of him," the bartender said. "You guys want a drink or are you on duty. Not that that ever matters." He reached under the bar momentarily and a small red light came on at the corner of the bar.

"We're private but just want to talk to Tony about a case we're working on."

A large, well-dressed man walked out of a room in the rear of the bar and up to the two detectives.

"Hey, I know you," he said to Homes. "You used to be on the Roswell force and helped the Atlanta boys down here sometimes. I know you, too," he said to Jack. "You're the drunk cop from Roswell."

Jack just smiled back at the man. "I'm no longer a cop or a drunk but I do work in Roswell. We're trying to find Tony Corona. He may know something about a case we're working on."

The man waited a moment, then nodded to the bartender who poured him a drink. "You'd think that cut on your head would have convinced you to keep your nose out of other people's business," he said to Homes. "Tony don't come in here no more. And he don't like cops almost as much as we don't like cops, private or not." He downed the drink in one swallow. "Now why don't you two move your asses out of my place before you pick up a few more bruises?"

Homes and Jack looked at each other, nodded at the man, and walked out of The Inferno.

Back in their car, Homes said, "Jack, you know who that was?"

"No idea," Jack said. " I did notice the bulge under his left arm. I'm betting it was a .45."

Homes smiled. "You'd win your bet. That was Carmine Salerno, the head of the Appricio family in New York. Always carries a .45. Wonder what he's doing down here."

Jack had to laugh. "Don't these guys ever disappear? Don't they ever run out of relatives?"

"Italians? You're kidding," Homes said. "They'll be around forever. The thing that's always puzzled me is that they aren't the dumb characters we see in the movies. They're smart as hell and actually work hard at being criminals. They could do well running legit businesses and some of them do."

"Where to now?"

"Let's try Tony's apartment. We can tip him off that we were asking about him but I bet he just got a phone call from The Inferno."

Salerno's apartment was in a condo close to the middle of downtown Atlanta. Homes and Jack parked on the street and walked up to the building.

"This isn't exactly the Taj Mahal," Jack said.

"Tony has always kept a low profile," Homes said. "I think he's pretty well-off but he doesn't like to show it."

They looked for names on the entry buzzer but didn't see a Salerno listed.

"Just push the buzzer with no name," Homes said. "That'll be him."

The return buzzer sounded and the men walked into the condo hallway. "Tell me how you knew that buzzer was him," Jack said.

"Through guile and cunning," Homes answered, smiling. "I saw the apartment number on the note I got from my buddy on the force down here."

"I never knew you had guile and cunning," Jack said, laughing. "Why the hell didn't you tell me this fifteen years ago? We could have made a fortune in the detective business."

"We did make a fortune," Homes said. "It's lying at the bottom of our fish tank. By the way, what're the diamonds worth today?" They got into an elevator and pushed the number four button.

"Last I checked about three and a half million," Jack said.

"Then why the hell are we spending our valuable time visiting Italian gangsters?" Homes said, chuckling.

They walked down a hallway to Salerno's apartment and knocked.

"Come in, Homes. The door's not locked. I've been expecting you."

"I told you he'd be tipped off," Homes said, opening the door.

Salerno was sitting on the sofa in his living room, wearing a bathrobe and watching a baseball game. He didn't get up. The room was sparsely furnished with the bare essentials. Homes was right about Tony not showing off.

He looked at the two detectives. "Homes you're looking older. It's been a few years. How are things in Roswell? What the hell happened to your head?"

"I'm fine, Tony. But we miss seeing you spreading joy around the metropolis You look the same. I think you know how I got this thing on my head. It's what we want to talk to you about."

Salerno did not ask them to sit. "Yeah, I owe my good looks to clean living," he said. "Help yourself to a drink over there on the bar. I guess that guy with you is the drunken detective you used to work with."

"He got on the clean-living bandwagon, too, Tony. Probably the only thing you have in common. And we're still working together."

Salerno smiled. "I bet. So what's on your mind? I don't know nothin' about that Carstairs murder. That was before my time." He glanced at the game. "I bet a bundle on the Yankees. I keep missin' them Mickey Mantle days when I was a kid in New York. I'm a sucker for the old days."

"Glad you're keeping up with things, Tony. Actually, we're not here about the Carstairs thing. We hear there's a couple of muscle guys in town who may have been visiting my friend here and me. One of them probably gave me this." He pointed to his head. "Heard anything about them?"

Salerno grunted and turned off the TV. "Fuckin' Yankees are too far behind anyway. They need pitching. Homes, you and me go back a long ways. You always treated me decent and I gave you some good tips over the years. Here's another one. Get your ass out of this Carstairs thing. There's more shit in it than you know. It ain't worth it." Salerno lit a cigarette. "My doc tells me to stop smoking. I tell him I'm cutting back."

"Tony, I'm getting too old to be gunned down by a mob stooge outside a mall. You know I could have busted you and put you away a couple of times. Now I need you to be straight with me. I know you've heard there are some professional hitmen in town. If you know where these guys are, I want you to tell me."

Salerno finally stood up. He walked to the bar and filled a water glass half full of bourbon, then walked back to the sofa and sat down. He seemed to be pondering.

"I'm supposed to quit drinking, too. Homes, you know it ain't doin' me any good when you go askin' around about me where I hang out. It ruins my clean-living image." He put his drink down on the coffee table and reached over to a pad and pen and started writing.

"Do me a favor. Tear up the address I'm givin' you. Don't tell anyone we talked. I'd prefer to remain – what do you guys call it – incongruous?"

Homes and Jack smiled. "You mean incognito." Homes took the note from him.

"Yeah, whatever. Just forget you know me. We'll call it even. Oh, one other thing for old times. These guys you're looking for are the real deal. They know their business and they're being paid a shitload of dough to take both of you out. Permanently. They ain't from New York, either. I hear from out west. If you do try and find them make sure you're packin' and you've got a lot of friends with you, if you know what I mean."

"Got it," Homes said. "Thanks for the tip, Tony. We're square and I won't mention your name to anyone."

The two men turned and left the apartment.

Homes was thoughtful as they drove away. "Those guys are funny. Cops joke about their so-called personal mob codes. But they do have them. And one of the big ones is paying back a debt even when they know it's dangerous to do it."

Jack nodded. "He seemed to know all about us and what we're doing. Neither one of us mentioned Carstairs but he was completely up to date."

"The Italian grapevine is still as good as it gets, partner. Now, do we head straight for the address Tony gave us or what?"

Jack thought a minute. "Well, we can't get FBI or police help based on absolutely no evidence. Are you okay if we go back home, pick up Diane, and then give the address a try? We know there's at least two guys, maybe more."

"If it comes to that, I'd take Diane in a shoot-out anytime. Let's try it."

17

"**H**ow do you want to handle this, guys?" Diane said.

"It's good and dark now. How about Homes and I hit the front of their place and you watch the back. I think we'll all get plenty of action," Jack said.

"Okay by me," Diane said. "I'm locked and loaded."

Homes chuckled. "They teach you that military talk in the FBI academy?"

"No, I was watching *Full Metal Jacket* on TV last night."

"That was a tough movie," Jack said. "Kept me from signing up with the Marines."

The team was headed to an address is south Atlanta in what the local PD called a Code Red neighborhood. It was just south of Carver High School near the DOJ Prison System.

"Think these bozos know how close they are to the prison?" Homes asked.

"Probably have lots of relatives inside," Diane said, grinning.

"Let's make sure we give them plenty of time together," Jack added. "Everybody got their vests on, plenty of spare ammo and your night vision goggles handy?"

"Yeah, I'm cool," Diane said. "So is the old dude sitting next to me." She patted Homes on his shoulder.

They drove slowly past the address and parked a block away, slightly around a corner. There were very few lights on in the neighborhood and none at all inside the target house. Using hand signals, Jack and Homes approached the front of the house while Diane trotted around the back. The men waited until she had time to set up at the back door.

"I suppose you want me to kick in the door," Homes whispered.

"That's right. With your head shaved you look the scariest."

"I love your sense of humor when we're about the get our asses shot off," Homes said.

"Let's go."

Homes kicked the door in, yelling out *"Atlanta PD. We got a warrant."* Not exactly true but he figured the department would cover for him.

The first shot rang out as they stepped inside, crouching low. At least one of their suspects was hidden behind a sofa which had been knocked over and used as a barricade.

Jack pointed to his goggles and then to the man behind the sofa and gave Homes a thumbs up, meaning the guy had night vision goggles, too, so both sides could see in the dark. Tony Salerno wasn't kidding. These guys were pros and ready for them. Jack and Homes shot at both ends of the sofa and waited. Homes was using a Luger semi-auto pistol with 20 rounds. He aimed a burst at the center of the sofa. They heard a cry followed by the sound of a weapon hitting the floor. Jack shook his head at Homes. If these guys were pros this might be all a part of the game. Nobody moved. Homes nodded.

Jack detached a few small smoke pellets from his belt and heaved them in the general direction of the sofa. Then both men crawled toward it, firing their weapons simultaneously. They were pros, too. There were no further sounds as they flipped the sofa over and saw the body. Jack put a round in the man's head and they both waited. Finally he and Homes raised up cautiously and looked around.

"Clear back here." They heard Diane's voice from the back of the house. "Clear up front," Homes yelled. "We're coming back."

The team came together and checked the rest of the house.

"Maybe the other guys went out to get a pizza," Homes said.

"Or they may be out looking for us," Jack said.

"So they could be coming back," Diane said. "This guy on the floor has a radio. They probably check in regularly and he's not going to answer when they do. So do we wait or get the hell out of here?"

"I vote that we go home and hunker down," Homes said. "Better yet, let's get a couple of rooms at a motel. Some place they'd least expect us."

"We passed one a mile back," Jack said. "You think they'd look for us in the neighborhood?"

"You two are both nuts. We're staying in an apartment with cameras and alarms all over the damned place and we're well-armed. Your place is comfortable, clean and close."

"And it has beer," Homes said.

"I was going to say that" Diane chuckled. "Let's head for home."

18

"**I** made you some coffee," Homes said, handing Diane a cup across the bed.

"A girl could get used to this kind of living," she said. "A night out on the town killing a hitman, then coffee in bed the next morning. This is the life."

"Wait. What about that night of incredible sex?" Homes said.

"You must have been dreaming, my friend. You feel asleep as soon as we got back."

"Well it was a damn good dream. Glad you were in it."

Diane grunted. "I need to go by my place and pick up some more clothes. Want to come?"

"Sure. You're not going to start covering yourself up with any pajamas are you?"

Diane smiled. "What you see is what you're gonna get."

"Well, I like what I see," Homes said, reaching for her.

"Gotta take a shower detective Kinney," she said, dodging his arms and sliding out of bed. "Check in with me later." She headed for the bathroom.

"I'll do that," he said, raising his voice.

"If you two are finished messing around, I made some breakfast out here," Jack yelled.

Homes walked out of his bedroom looking disappointed.

"It can't be that bad," Jack said. "And you might as well get used to it. This is what happens when you get married. Have you asked her yet?"

"No, not yet. Don't rush me, will ya?"

"Rush you? How many weeks has it been since you first told me? What the hell are you waiting for?"

"The right time. I'll know it when it comes."

Jack laughed. "You're not getting any younger, my friend."

"Neither are you," Homes said. "By the way, when are you getting married.?"

"I'm waiting for the right woman. Have some eggs."

The two men were eating breakfast when Diane walked out of the bedroom with one towel wrapped around her body and another around her hair.

"Gee, thanks for waiting, gentlemen. Did you leave me anything to eat?"

"There's a package of kale in the frig," Homes said. " I was saving it for some of that Vietnamese stuff you're fixing for dinner. Jack and I are eating out."

"Don't get me involved in this squabble. I love Vietnamese food," Jack said.

"He's just mad because he didn't get laid last night," Diane said. "Poor baby. Besides, this is one Vietnamese that doesn't eat kale."

Homes' cell phone buzzed cutting off what he hoped was going to be a smartass answer to Diane.

"Yeah, Kinney," he said. "I'd know that voice anywhere, Cap. How are you doin'? Jack, It's Captain Taylor."

"That's what I was going to ask you," Taylor said. "I have a feeling you boys have been busy. I got a call from Fred Barzell at Atlanta PD. He tells me they found a guy that's on their hot list that was shot a couple of times in a house down by the federal prison. From the way he's dressed and the night vision specs he was wearing he's definitely a pro. Might that be your handiwork?"

"I cannot tell a lie, Chief. I know nothing about that."

"I thought you'd say that. This is just a heads up that Barzell has his eyes on you two and a tip that he says there are two more of these guys out there. So keep your eyes open."

"Always do, Cap," Homes said. "I appreciate you looking out for us."

"Homes, I've got another reason for calling that may or may not tie in with hitmen in the area. A woman in Roswell was murdered in her apartment last night. I think you were asking about her a week or so ago. Name was Amber Still. Street name of Dyno Mite. She took two in the chest. Apartment has been torn to shit. They were obviously looking for something important."

"Oh, hell," Homes said. " I was just talking to her about the Carstairs case. She was picked up a couple of times for prostitution in the old days. Can I still get into the crime scene?"

"Sure. You know the address?"

"Yeah, I got that. Thanks for cluing me in, Cap. I'll let you know if I find out anything."

He hung up. "Well, now we know where the other two gunmen were last night. They paid a visit to Amber Still, one of the women I talked to about the Carstairs murder. Shot in the chest. Apartment ransacked. I'm heading over there."

"How about if I join you?" Jack said. "I've got nothing going on right now."

"Great. Just let me get some clothes on."

"I'll stay here and get dressed, guys," Diane said. "Then I've got a few phone calls to make."

"Okay, we'll be back in an hour or so."

◆ ◆ ◆

"Wonder what they were looking for in her place?" Jack said.

"Beats me. Maybe dope. Amber was a drunk and a junkie. Harmless as far as I could tell. Jack, I'm more than fed up with all this killing. We need to stop this shit." He pulled up at their apartment. Diane's car was gone.

"Thought she said she was making phone calls," Jack said.

"Yeah. She told me earlier she needed to go back to her place and pick up more clothes. I told her I'd go with her. Then all this other stuff happened." They walked into their apartment.

Homes headed for the kitchen. "Here's a note. Says she's gone to get clothes. Back in a half-hour. Time on the note is 9:30."

"It's almost noon now," Jack said. "And you never got a call from her?"

"No. Nothin'. This doesn't feel right. Let's get over to her place."

Homes broke every traffic law getting over to Diane's apartment. Her car was parked outside. The two men ran up to the second floor.

"I don't have a key," Homes said as he knocked, then pounded on the door. "I'm crashin' in, Jack."

"I'm with you." They both kicked hard on the door and it gave quickly. There were two bodies on the floor. One of them was Diane. Shattered furniture was scattered all over the living room, a broken mirror on one wall.

"Oh, Jesus," Homes shouted as he rushed over and knelt beside her. "If she's gone I'm going to tear this town apart." He checked her carotid for a pulse. "She's still breathing and I don't see any blood. Hell of a lump on her head. You better call –"

"I'm already on it. 911's on the way. I also called the FBI and Roswell PD."

Jack walked over to the other body. It was a man wearing the same outfit and gear as the character they had shot the night before. A knife was buried in his chest. Jack pulled off his ski mask and saw he was covered with bruises and had lost a couple of teeth. One arm was badly twisted and had a broken wrist. The man's weapon lay beside him.

"Jesus, Holmes. He looks like somebody beat the shit out of him."

"That was no somebody. It was Diane. That knife in his heart is her Gerber."

"Her what?"

"Her Gerber combat knife. Given to her by her father. Wears it in a sheath on her right ankle. Never goes anywhere without it. Except to bed, of course. Deadly as hell when she needs it to be and that's obviously what she was going for. It's called don't fuck with the Vietnamese."

"Right. If this guy jumped her when she walked in she probably didn't have time to pull her Glock. Bet he didn't know he was in for the fight of his life."

Then they heard sirens getting closer.

19

"She's got a mild concussion and some other bruises but she'll be fine," the doctor said. "Are you a relative," he asked Homes.

"Fiancé," he said. "You're sure she's –"

"I'm sure. We'll keep a close watch on her because of the concussion. You can go in and see her but don't stay long."

Homes and Jack walked into Diane's room. Her eyes were closed and she looked like a little girl with her head wrapped in a bandage. One hand was also covered. The entire right side of her face was black and blue. Homes bent over and held her hand. She opened her eyes.

"This rough sex isn't all it's cracked up to be," she said, trying to smile.

"Why didn't you –"

"I thought I was only going to be gone for a while and it was broad daylight. I know better than to take chances like that. Now I'll get chewed out by Sheppard and the rest of the guys in the office."

"I called Bob, Diane. So you can expect a visit soon."

"Good, Thanks, Jack. Geeze, this hurts like hell."

"Didn't they give you anything –"

"I don't take drugs, Homes. Not any drugs for any reason. You know that."

"Yeah." He smiled down at her. "I forgot."

"I'm going to leave you two alone," Jack said, walking out. "I'll see you later, Diane."

The two lovers looked at each other without speaking for several minutes.

"Now you know how it feels," Diane said.

"What . . . ? "

"When the person you love is almost killed," she said. "This is how I felt when you were shot."

"This is the worst I've ever felt in my life. Even worse than when I shot Jack to save his life."

Diane smiled at him. "It's over now and I need to sleep. Go home and have a beer."

Jack stuck his head in the door. "Roswell PD is sending two men to sit outside your door 24/7. I think your guys at the FBI will also have it covered. We'll leave when they arrive." He closed the door.

"Diane, can I ask you one thing before I go?"

"He never touched me, Homes. I mean he never got to me – you know –"

"I know. That's not it." He took a deep breath. "Diane, will you marry me? I don't have a ring yet but –"

"Oh, shut up," she said, trying not to cry. "Of course I'll marry you."

◆ ◆ ◆

"I think we need to change our strategy." Homes was pissed. "The woman I'm going to marry was almost killed. ME – I was almost killed. Jack here was almost killed. What has to happen before we all get more serious about this whole Carstairs thing? Especially you, Sheppard, and the whole goddamn FBI."

Sheppard was quiet for a moment. He looked briefly at Jack, then at Homes.

"We got formal permission today to raid Breckenridge and collect everything. That's happening now, as we sit here. The attack on Diane in her own apartment and the severe injuries she suffered changed the whole picture in Washington. Like everyone else in law enforcement, we take attacks on our own people very seriously. I'm sorry that it took something like this. I also want you to know that we're trying to identify who exactly pulled the plug on this investigation to begin with. You'd think that would be easy to determine but it's not. Nobody's talking. But we'll get there."

"I think we're past the point where we can just smile and say thank you, Bob," Jack said. "This became pretty serious to us the more we dug into it and then the shooting and killing started. We're way beyond the time when people should have started being arrested. Will that happen today?"

"The arrests? Probably not," Sheppard said. "But the information you and Homes have already provided, along with whatever we pick up today, ought to make that happen pretty soon."

"Great. What do we – Homes and Diane and I – do in the meantime? Do we just barricade ourselves in our apartment and wait for the next attack? I mean, this is bullshit, Bob, and you know it."

Sheppard nodded. "I agree, Jack, and I've apologized to you already for the way the FBI has handled this. It is not our usual procedure as you well know. That's part of the problem – running into these frustrating slowdowns and stops from Washington. But that appears to be over now. In the meantime you can count on us supplying protection for all of you on a 24-hour basis. That can include moving you all to a safehouse if you think that's necessary."

"Maybe we should all change our names and move to another state. Or country," Homes said, not smiling.

A man entered the room with a note for Sheppard. "This is the latest update on Diane. She's doing much better. No repercussions from the concussion. They think she can be released tomorrow."

"That's the first good news we've had in a hell of a long time," Homes said, slamming his hand down on the table.

"We'll have a group of agents there when they let her go."

"Jack and I will be there, I can tell you that, whether or not your guys show up. I'm through playing games with this whole operation." Homes stood up. "Let's get out of this chicken-shit place, Jack." The two men left Sheppard's office and the FBI building.

"Let's go get some lunch," Jack said as they drove back toward Roswell.

"Gee, you think it's safe?" Homes said facetiously. "I'm getting tired of looking over our shoulders. I feel like we're back in Vietnam and heading into Laos to look for your dad."

"I know the feeling," Jack said. "But I'll be damned if we're going to start being afraid of our shadows."

20

"We can pick her up in an hour but I want to go over early," Homes said.

"Fine with me," Jack said, as he finished cleaning his father's .45. "We can talk more as we drive over but I hope you'll give some thought to you and Diane getting out of here for a while. I mean going somewhere you can relax and not deal with all this shit."

Homes nodded as he stood up. "I know what you're saying and I'm tempted to go along with it. But as stubborn as I am about finishing a case, especially this one, Diane is even more so. I'll suggest it to her but I don't think she's going to back off because of what's happened to all three of us. She'll want to stay and finish the job. But I'll ask her."

The drive to the hospital only took ten minutes. They spotted the Roswell PD and FBI agents outside Diane's hospital room right away.

"I'll wait out here," Jack said. "Why don't you go into her room and help her with her stuff."

Homes went inside and found Diane arguing with a nurse about not needing a wheelchair to leave the hospital. "I'm not a cripple," she said, "and I'll be damned if I'm going to let those agents outside see me in a wheelchair."

"Sounds like you're feeling better," Homes said, smiling and giving her a careful hug. "Diane, you know these hospital rules. It's standard procedure. I had to sit in one of those damn things when I got out of here a few weeks ago. They won't let you go unless you do it."

"I'd like to see them stop me," she said, picking up the few items she had in the room.

Her doctor came in and smiled. "Anxious to get out of here, I see. Things will go a lot faster if you'll follow our hospital's safety policy."

Diane picked up her cell phone and pressed a number. "Bob, it's Diane. I'm fine. Please call off the two guys you have outside my room so I can get out of here. I've had all the shit I can take since this happened and I don't want any of our guys giving me even more because I had to be rolled out in a wheelchair. Yes, Homes and Jack are here and so are two Roswell PD officers. Good. Thanks. I'm on my way. Call you when we get home."

"Okay, here's the deal," Diane said to the doctor. "My boss is going to relieve the two agents outside the door. When they're gone I'll agree to sit in the wheelchair while I'm rolled out to the front door. Will that satisfy everyone?"

The doctor nodded. "Nurse, why don't you wait outside until the FBI agents depart. Then come back in and help Ms. Nguyen pack up and leave."

Homes and Jack walked alongside Diane in the wheelchair as they headed for the exit. Both men were armed and Diane had received her Glock from hospital security. The two Roswell PD officers walked ahead of them and checked the outside of the hospital. No one was taking any chances.

With Diane safely in the car, two Roswell PD vehicles signaled Jack and one pulled out ahead of him while the second pulled in behind him. The three friends drove out of the parking lot and headed safely for home.

"Nice to see you so agreeable back in the hospital this morning, Diane," Jack said, chuckling.

"I hate hospitals," she said, leaning over and giving Homes a peck on the cheek.

"I don't want you two making out in the back seat while I'm driving," Jack said, trying to lighten the mood. "It's distracting and it's turning me on."

"That's your problem," Diane said, giving Homes a sexier kiss. "That's as much as you're going to get, baby," she said, "until I get over some of these bruises."

"I'm glad you're a fast healer," he said, "so I know I won't have to wait long."

Jack laughed as they pulled into their apartment parking area. "You lovebirds wait a minute while we wait for the Roswell boys to check things out before we go inside."

Homes grunted. "They damn sure ought to be here. Roswell got us into this situation to begin with."

After a signal from the officers checking the outside of their apartment, they walked slowly from the car to the entrance of their home, with Diane in between the two men. They made it inside the apartment without incident. Jack reset all the appropriate surveillance devices and alarms while Diane called Sheppard and told him she was safe, thanking him for his security team at the hospital.

"I'm ready for a beer," Homes said. "Diane?"

"I need an uninterrupted nap," she said, "in that nice bed of yours where I won't be interrupted every ten minutes to have my temperature checked." She gave both men a hug and headed for the bedroom. "Let's talk later."

Jack and Homes sat down at their conference table. "She's pretty tough," Jack said, "but I knew that."

"Yeah. I'll ask her about taking a trip when she's had a good rest but I think I know what she's going to say."

Jack nodded. "And I think you're right. Can't hurt to ask, though. Is there anything else you want to do on the case that we can handle without getting killed? We ought to have a report from Sheppard sometime soon about what they were able to get out of the Breckenridge raid."

"Right," Homes said, sipping on his beer. "I guess we sit tight until then. I'm anxious to get this over with."

"What do you think about any remaining shooters who may be out there? I know we can't account for at least one."

"Doesn't matter," Homes said. "By this time whoever is behind this could have called up a half-dozen other bad asses to nail us."

"True," Jack said. "At least we've got FBI and Roswell police watching our place twenty-four seven."

◆ ◆ ◆

Later that afternoon the fax machine in their office hummed into action. It was a concise report about the Breckenridge raid. Both men read it carefully and remarked about the last sentence. *Arrest warrants have been issued for Arnold Folkman, Donald Carstairs, Alice Townsend, Maxine Turner, Rudy Simmons, and Audrey Taylor.*

"I was hoping Alice wouldn't be on that list," Jack said. "It's a damn shame."

"I feel the same way about Audrey Taylor," Homes said. "I don't know what they've got on her but I hope she comes out of this okay."

"I see they used both names for Donald Carstairs. The FBI is always efficient."

"I'm still not ready to pat them on the back," Homes said. "Have you heard anything from Washington about why they shut the investigation down?"

"No, nothing. Sheppard may have picked something up. We'll find out later."

The door to Homes' bedroom opened and a still-sleepy Diane walked out rubbing her eyes. "Was that a fax machine I heard?" she said.

They handed her the FBI report and she sat down at the conference table.

"Isn't Simmons the baseball player?" she asked. "How is he involved in this?"

"We're not sure," Jack said. "But the Breckenridge computer guy, Robert Sawyer, said his name showed up several times with payoffs for undefined reasons."

Diane stretched and stood up. "I'd love to join my guys when the arrests are made in a day or two but right now I'm headed back to bed."

21

J ack was sitting at his desk going over old case reports when his phone rang. Homes and Diane had gone out to dinner, accompanied by the now-familiar Roswell police escort.

"Jack, it's Alice. "I've been thinking over what we talked about the last time we were together. Can you come over tonight? I've changed my mind about several things."

"Funny, but I've been sitting here listening to one of your albums and working, worried about how you would handle the FBI arrest warrants. I'm assuming you know about them even if they haven't been served yet. Sure, I can stop by. I have some suggestions for you that might be helpful. Is around seven a good time?"

"I need all the help I can get," she said. "Seven is perfect. I'll even feed you a snack or two."

Jack smiled as he put his cell back on the table. He was having trouble getting Alice out of his mind and worrying more about what could happen to her legally and financially. With Homes and Diane out for the evening he had nothing planned and seeing Alice again was just what he needed. As he left the apartment he walked over to the Roswell police car parked outside. The officer inside was an old friend from Jack's days on the force.

"Hey, Fred. I see you got stuck with baby-sitting tonight."

"Hi, Jack. Yeah, but it's for a good cause. How are you and Homes doing?"

"We're good. Homes is out on a date and I'm about to do the same. I have to drive downtown. How about if you shadow me to where I'm going and then take the night off?"

Fred laughed. "Hey, buddy, I'd love to help you out but you know how the Cap is about his direct orders. His order to me was to not let you out of my sight for any reason."

"I remember those orders very well and I understand. Look, I expect to be spending the night where I'm headed and won't come back until early morning. You can wait outside this condo all night if you want. Just don't expect me to come out until about six am."

"Got it. That's cool. As long as I know where you are. Good luck tonight," Fred said, smiling."

"Thanks buddy. I'll tell the Cap you were a real pain in the ass."

◆ ◆ ◆

Alice must have been standing at the door to her apartment because she opened it just as he knocked. They quickly embraced and made the moment last.

"It's good to feel you again," he said, pressing against her.

"That feeling's mutual." She kissed him a little longer then led him to the sofa. "You know the fact that you don't drink is saving me a great deal of money. I've become more conscious of my spending since your warning." She was smiling.

"I'm glad. I was serious when I told you that you didn't have to worry about money. I'm in pretty good shape financially and I'll cover whatever you need. I also have some good friends among Atlanta's top attorneys if you find you need one."

She was silent for a moment. "I hope that won't be necessary, Jack, but I appreciate the thought, especially for the monetary help. As you know, I'm a very expensive girl."

"I know. And worth every penny," he said as the reached for her.

"I think that's quite enough foreplay." The voice was not one Jack recognized. He pulled away from Alice and started to reach for the weapon in his shoulder holster.

"I wouldn't do that, Mr. Novak. While I do intend to exterminate you, I'd prefer not to shoot you in Alice's apartment. Certainly not on her lovely sofa. Blood stains are so hard to remove from Italian silk. Alice, get his gun."

She did as she was told. "I'm sorry, Jack," she said, taking his weapon.

"I'm betting you're Donald Carstairs," Jack said, looking up at the man, "or should I call you Arnold Folkman? You really are a dead ringer for your brother."

"Appropriate language for Duane, Mr. Novak, since he departed from this world some time ago. And not accidentally, as you've probably guessed by now. He was such a stupid man but a perfect front for our business before his drug and sex habits made him unreliable. I had to dispose of him myself which was actually quite pleasant. I'm sure you're curious about many things and we do have a few reasons for keeping you alive. At least for the time being."

"That's good to hear," Jack said. He glanced at Alice who had stood up and walked over next to Donald. "What's Alice's role in all this?"

"As she told me you suggested to her, Alice has been most helpful in what you law and order types call laundering money. I prefer calling it exchanging funds. By the way, Alice's sexual involvement with you was at my direction. She's really very good, isn't she? Why don't we sit over there, my dear," he said, "where I can keep closer watch on Mr. Novak." He patted her arm while she placed Jack's gun in her purse.

"Are you two –"

Carstairs smiled. "Are we lovers? Not for some time. A long time, actually. While Alice is a delightful woman, and I love listening to her voice, I prefer her financial services. I was always intrigued by her – oh, her involvement with my brother's wife, Wendy. Wendy and I were lovers although love had nothing to do with it. I found her various vices intriguing and our physical relationship allowed me to keep a closer eye on my brother. Alice has only one vice that I know of. Living the good life and that requites money." He patted her arm again.

"Look, Carstairs, the feds and local law enforcement have finished building a case against you and your friends. You can't get away with whatever you're planning."

"Dear me, Mr. Novak. You sound like a 1940s movie detective. I've taken care of the federal gendarmes as I'm sure you know. I know the FBI has issued warrants but they haven't been served as yet. And I do intend to get away from all of this scot-free. You and your friend Mr. Kinney are only minor irritations and will both be taken care of. I do regret that the individuals who were supposed to shoot and kill you and Kinney missed their mark. I eliminated the last of them immediately. The same is true for the two miscreants who were supposed to dispose of you on the highway. I do not stand for incompetence by anyone in my employ. I have also reinforced those original guns-for-hire with some more efficient thugs."

"Alice, you don't need to do this –"

"Come now, Mr. Novak. I expected more from you. Ms. Townsend's twenty or more years of working within our little enterprise have been carefully documented. Should anything happen to me, detailed information about her involvement will be distributed to the pertinent government agencies, as well as to the media. She must be completely loyal to me whether she likes it or not. And now I grow weary of this distraction. Will you proceed with our plan for Mr. Novak, my dear?"

Carstairs handed Alice a pair of handcuffs and she walked toward Jack who was still sitting on the sofa.

"Jack, I have no choice," she whispered to him.

"We all have choices," he said, as she snapped the handcuffs onto his wrists. She walked over to a living room table and opened the center drawer, withdrawing a small rectangular black box With her other hand she picked up a bottle of bourbon and walked back to him.

"This is a dreadful waste of expensive bourbon," Carstairs said as Alice poured it over Jack. "It will serve our purpose if anyone should interrupt us as we leave. You see, I know a great deal about you, Mr. Novak, and your longtime alcoholism. I was surprised to learn of your other addiction to even heavier drugs a few years ago but that may come in handy as well."

"Many people know where I am and what I'm doing, Carstairs. Leaving a trail of dead bodies isn't going to help your cause."

"Oh, there will be no bodies, Mr. Novak. Not even a trace. I assume there will be inquiries after you, your partner and his attractive Asian woman are reported missing. They will produce nothing. You may inject him now, my dear," Carstairs said.

Alice opened the black box and withdrew a hypodermic, filling it about a third full of a clear liquid from a vial also in the box.

"Have no fear, Mr. Novak, at least not for the immediate present. This injection will not kill you but only make you more pliable and reasonable as we leave here in a moment."

"Where to?" Jack asked as he winced from the injection.

"Not that it matters," Carstairs said, "but we are going to the Breckenridge building to finish our little business. I have a private office in the basement. It's soundproof," he said, smiling. "You see, Maxine Turner and several other – uh – employees informed me that you have Wendy Carstairs' diary, the contents of which might prove – difficult – for me. I didn't know it existed or I would have had her disposed of even earlier than I ordered it done. Before this night is over I can promise you that you will reveal the diary's whereabouts to me."

22

Jack was never entirely unconscious as he, Carstairs and Alice made the short drive to Breckenridge headquarters. The handcuffs remained tightly around his wrists. He could catch snatches of conversation as he faded in and out. The smell of bourbon actually kept his senses sharper than they would have been.

He felt the car slow down, then heard someone say . . . *The code is nine-three-six-zero,* followed by the sound of a garage door slowly rising. The car drove into what Jack assumed was the basement of Breckenridge and stopped. His door opened and he was pulled out by two men wearing face masks and dragged across the floor and into what looked like a large office, brightly lit. He could hear Carstairs and Alice talking and following closely behind him. Still groggy, he was forced to sit in a chair while his arms were tied to the chair-back and he had a chance to look around the room. There were several desks arranged haphazardly, complete with computers and telephones. At one of the desks sat Rudy Simmons, the former baseball player, who was on his cell phone. There were no windows. Except for a few extra chairs, the rest of the room was barren.

"I hope you are comfortable, Mr. Novak," Donald Carstairs said, walking toward him. "I think you know Mr. Simmons who appears to be involved on the phone. You can speed up the inevitable by telling me now where Wendy's diary is located. Oh, we know you were accompanied by a police vehicle to Ms. Townsend's condominium but we left that building by the rear service exit so he has no knowledge that you are gone. There are no rescuers you can count on. Now, about the diary . . ."

Jack was still sluggish from whatever drug Alice had given him but he was aware of what was happening. He realized that even if he told Carstairs there was no real diary, and that he had just made up the story, no one would believe him. He decided to remain silent.

"I must warn you, Mr. Novak, that my patience is extremely limited. Let me give you some encouragement." Carstairs walked up to Jack and slapped him hard, twice, across the face. Jack strained his arms against the ropes.

"I usually enjoy giving physical punishment but my time is short and I have other plans. Tell me what I want to know now or, when your friends arrive, I will turn my attention to Ms. Nguyen and I will not be gentle,"

Jack said nothing.

The door to the office opened abruptly and two more masked men pushed Homes and Diane into the room. They were both handcuffed and didn't appear to be drugged. The men forced them into chairs across from Jack and tied their arms back. Then they left the room.

"Jack, are you okay?" Homes said. "What the fuck is -"

Carstairs reached across and slapped Homes hard. "Please be quiet Mr. Kinney. We have no time for conversation. I do apologize for my men interrupting your romantic dinner. There is only one reason for all of you to still be alive. I have an urgent need to recover Wendy Carstairs' diary. You are all going to die in any case. But you can spare yourselves harsh interrogation with extreme pain if you will simply tell me what I want to know. To speed up this procedure, if one of you does not tell me, I will begin my cross examination with Ms. Nguyen. I can promise you that it will be extremely prolonged and painful. She does have lovely eyes, doesn't she? I noticed them right away when I first saw her. That's what gave me this idea."

"Diane doesn't know anything," Homes said. "Leave her alone."

"Do your damndest," Diane spat. "I have a very high threshold for pain."

"Not this kind of pain, my dear." Carstairs reached into his jacket pocket and pulled out a small vial. "I doubt that any of you have ever heard of Aqua Regia. It is a combination of hydrochloric and nitric acids. This glass vial with the lovely yellow-orange color holds it safely but very little else can. Aqua

Regia can instantly dissolve solid gold and platinum. Just one powerful drop can penetrate virtually anything. But if someone should carelessly add a drop to – let's say a human eye – oh, my goodness." Carstairs smiled broadly. "The acid will instantly penetrate the eye, then the brain and on to the top of the spinal cord. It can't be stopped."

Homes' face was bright red. "I told you she doesn't know anything about a diary."

"What she actually knows doesn't matter," Carstairs said, ignoring him. "Either you, Mr. Kinney, or Mr. Novak, have the answer and you will both have the dubious pleasure of watching Ms. Nguyen experience pain and torment beyond her wildest imagination. We'll see just how high her so-called threshold really is. You are all intelligent people and you must realize that a quick and painless death is preferable to a torturous one. Oh, did I say as the acid slowly dissolves and moves from place to place in her eye, then her brain, the pain will be excruciating. Then she will die."

The door to the room opened again and Maxine Taylor, Breckenridge's COO, joined the group.

"Maxine, my dear, so nice to see you and to have you with us. I want to thank you again for advising me of Wendy's diary after your conversation with Mr. Kinney."

Taylor looked around the room. "What's she doing here?" She nodded toward Alice.

"Oh, Ms. Townsend has been an essential part of the plan to lure Mr. Novack here. She has done her job well using her obvious provocative talents." Carstairs smiled.

"I've told you before that I hated her and never wanted to see her again. She not only corrupted Duane and Wendy, she has never really been a part of our core business."

"Maxine, we do not have time for these petty jealousies," Carstairs said, glaring at her. "You have all been valuable players and I consider every one of you to be an essential worker."

"That woman forced Duane into using drugs and that led to his –" she was trying to find the right word – "to his preoccupation with sluts and tramps." There were tears in her eyes.

"I have never used drugs in my life," Alice said. "Duane was an addict and an immoral and salacious man. He was also a fool. You were in love with him and he resisted all your attempts to seduce him, if you even know how."

"YOU BITCH," Maxine shouted and moved toward Alice.

"This nonsense must stop immediately," Carstairs announced. "Maxine, I promoted you to head Breckenridge after I disposed of Duane and made you a rich woman. You have no reason to have hard feelings for Alice."

"You . . . you dis – you killed Duane?" she stuttered.

"It was unavoidable. I did it to save the organization and all of you," he said. "Now let's move on."

"What about Wendy?" Homes interrupted. "Did you kill Wendy, too?"

"Don't be absurd," Carstairs said. "Our baseball friend over there –" he pointed to Rudy Simmons – "did that job quite nicely with a little help from his friends. Isn't that right, Rudy?"

Simmons smiled and walked toward the group. "It was no big thing. The Carstairs bitch told me we were through. She said that bastard Booster Desmond was better in the sack than me. I knew that was a lie and no bitch dumps Rudy Simmons. So when Carstairs here asked me to do the deed and that he would put me on the payroll, I said sure. I had one more last roll with that red-headed whore and heard her beggin' for more. Then I fixed her a special - oh, a *cocktail* - if you know what I mean. She loved havin' sex on drugs. I shot her up and watched her fade away." Simmons smiled and shrugged.

"Rudy, you didn't need Carstairs' money. Why –" Jack was stunned.

"Hey, man. I was bettin' and losin' – bigtime. I bet on my team and every other damn thing. I was into the sharks – the loan sharks - for over a million. Carstairs gave me a way out. Besides, there are lots of Wendys and only one Rudy Simmons." He smiled. "I gave some friends a taste of that special white stuff Wendy was so fond of and they handled all that fancy stabbing. And how did you like my idea of slicin' that chick's head off and leaving it in a dumpster in Roswell park? Made it look like one a them cults did it to her. They'll never figure that one out cause none of you will ever talk."

"She wasn't a bitch," Alice said. "She was a lovely and sensuous woman." Alice had tears in her eyes. "I had no idea that you killed her, Rudy. I thought it was Donald." She stared angrily at Carstairs.

"STOP IT," Carstairs shouted. "You are all fools. We are here to find Wendy's diary, which mentions all of our names and describes our duties – our CRIMINAL duties - within the company. THAT is what is important now, not all of this ridiculous history. Rudy, tie up Ms. Nguyen's legs. She will be unable to stop thrashing around once I begin." He withdrew the vial again from his pocket.

"You killed him . . . you killed Duane . . . " Maxine kept repeating the phrase over and over, as if she were in a trance. She reached slowly into the pocket of her smock and pulled out a .38 revolver. "You killed Duane," she said, pointing the gun at Carstairs, who was staring at the tools.

"NO, LADY! NO." Rudy Simmons yelled out as he saw her weapon. "Jesus, don't."

They heard a shot and Carstairs slumped to the floor, a surprised look on his face.

The second shot also came from Maxine as she held the gun to her head and pulled the trigger.

"This shit has got to stop," Rudy said, pulling his own gun, the gold-plated .45 he had shown Jack in his apartment.

"No, it is about time you were stopped, you arrogant bastard." It was Alice Townsend who still had Jack's gun in her purse and was now pointing it at Rudy. Rudy swiveled his weapon toward Alice. They both fired at about the same time.

"Oh, God, no," Jack moaned as he tried to get out of his chair. He watched the blood pouring from Alice's chest as she lay on the floor. Rudy was trying to crawl over to the group and drew his last breath as he reached toward them.

"Who's got the keys to these damned things?" Homes said, struggling with his cuffs.

"They're probably on Carstairs," Diane said, still cuffed.

"Alice had them last," Jack said. "And that's my gun she used."

"I can get to her," Diane said, standing up and dragging her chair over to Homes. "Honey, can you pull my knife out of the sheath on my ankle and run it through these ropes?" She lifted her right leg up to his hands and he finally was able to pull it free and began to saw through her ropes. When she was free she walked over to Alice and her open purse on the floor and found the keys.

"That's great, baby," Homes said. "It will be easier if you just drop them in my hands and let me fool with the damn things until I unlock my –"

"Way ahead of you, detective," Diane said, freeing her own wrists from her cuffs, and bending down to untie his. "We practiced this for hours in the academy," she said.

23

"We picked up Audrey Taylor the day after the murders," Sheppard said. "She was the only one left as far as we know. I asked her why her friend Amber Still had been murdered. She said Carstairs men were told Amber had a diary. Jack, I heard you and Homes mention a diary. What's that all about?"

Jack and Homes glanced at each other and shook their heads. "There was no diary. Homes and I made up a story about Wendy Carstairs' diary that mentioned all these people and what they were doing at Breckenridge. I guess we oversold it. Donald Carstairs was going to kill all three of us because of it."

"Amber didn't know shit about anything. Damn shame," Homes said. "Audrey was smart as hell and had a nice kid. Sorry she got involved in this mess."

"Guess she needed the money," Sheppard said. "She used that good brain of hers to set up one hell of a drug distribution system throughout Atlanta and the suburbs. And working in that drug rehab center gave her lots of information and contacts."

"With plenty of help from the late Rudy Simmons," Homes added.

"His connections with professional athletes sure didn't hurt," Diane agreed.

There was silence in the room.

"I guess you all know how lucky you were," Sheppard said. "From what you told me, that shoot-out must have looked like the wild west."

"Yeah, I thought for a while we were all going down. It was a hell of a thing." Homes said.

Jack tried to smile and failed. "At least we found out who murdered Wendy Carstairs. You can check that one off your bucket list, Homes."

"It ain't worth it," he said. "Too many murders."

"I understand congratulations are in order, Diane," Sheppard said. "That's a beautiful ring. The detective business must be picking up."

"Thanks, boss. Homes says he's had fifty-five years to save his money and claims he spent it all on this diamond." She waved her hand around. "Now he says it's my job to take care of him. I'm looking forward to it."

"Hey, why don't we go get some lunch," Jack said. "Homes is buying."

"I'll have to borrow some money from Diane," he said, grinning. "Where's the nearest McDonalds?"

◆ ◆ ◆

The two men stood looking at each other. Jack was standing next to his suitcase. Finally, he broke the silence.

"Homes, I can't remember how many times you've saved my ass."

"Well, at least you've saved mine once. I think I need a beer." He walked into the kitchen, pulled one from the fridge, and came back into the living room. "So what's next?"

Jack was uncomfortable. "Homes, I'm going to hang it up."

"Hang what up?"

"The detective business. All of it. I'm giving it to you."

Homes swallowed several times and looked at the beer bottle.

"What if I don't want it? I have other things to do."

Jack had to smile. "Like what?"

"I'm going to get married."

"So I've heard. Besides, that has nothing to do with running a detective business."

Homes thought about that. "So what are you going to do?"

"Nothing. I'm taking my half of the diamonds, converting a few of them for cash in Antwerp, then heading for the UAE."

"The United Arab Emirates, where Skinner lives?"

"Right. We've talked about flying over to see Skins. He's picked out an apartment for me in that expensive condo of his, complete with a – well, he says she's a housekeeper and cook." Jack chuckled.

"I bet. I'll just bet she cooks. And after that -?"

"After that, not a thing. I'm going to relax and live my life. I'm through with getting shot at and hit and getting closer every time to – well, to the last time. I lot of people got killed in this thing we just went through with Breckenridge. Some of them were decent even if they had their faults. I'm through with all of that kind of thing."

"Will you come back for my wedding? You're supposed to be the best man."

"I still don't think you'll go through with it but, yes, I'll come back and walk you down the aisle."

"I don't think the best man does that. That's the bride."

"You want me to walk the bride down the aisle?" Jack started laughing.

"No, stupid. Her father does that. You're supposed to take me out the night before and get me drunk and laid."

"Well, I do have a certain amount of experience in those two areas," Jack said. "What else?"

Homes thought a minute and drank the rest of his beer. "I think you pay for my tuxedo."

"Like hell. I'm leaving you almost two million dollars' worth of diamonds for God's sake. I'm not paying for your tuxedo."

"How about the liquor?"

"Yes, I'll pay for that."

"Will you get drunk with me?"

Jack laughed and shook his head. "What kind of a question is that for the recovering alcoholic you know so well? You've pulled me out of more drunken situations than I can count. So I'll just watch you get drunk."

"I was only kidding," Homes said. "Maybe we should both go to Antwerp so I can see how you turn the diamonds into cash. Diane can come and you can bring . . . whoever."

"It's *whomever*," Jack said. "Yes, we could do that."

"One last trip. Maybe one last case."

They were silent again. "Homes, I –"

"Don't start making speeches about how much our friendship has meant to you," Homes said.

"I was just going to say that you can have my car."

"I hate your car. It's too small."

"Diane can drive it."

"Diane says your car smells funny."

They stared at each other. "I have something to say," Homes said.

"Don't you start," Jack said, shaking his head.

"It's important."

"Okay, what is it.?"

"I think we're out of beer. You forgot to fill up the fridge."

The two friends hugged each other, both trying not to show the other what they were feeling.

"I'll be seeing you," Jack said.

"Not if I see you first," Homes said.

"Old joke," Jack said, turning his head away. "I'll miss those."

He picked up his suitcase and walked out of the apartment.